TREASURE OF THE DEAD

A DANE AND BONES ORIGIN STORY

DAVID WOOD
RICK CHESLER

Copyright

Published by Gryphonwood Press

ISBN-10: 1-940095-50-6
ISBN-13: 978-1-940095-50-9

Works by David Wood

The Dane Maddock Adventures

Dourado
Cibola
Quest
Icefall
Buccaneer
Atlantis
Ark

Dane and Bones Origins

Freedom
Hell Ship
Splashdown
Dead Ice
Liberty
Electra
Amber
Justice
Treasure of the Dead

Jade Ihara Adventures (with Sean Ellis)

Oracle
Changeling

Bones Bonebrake Adventures

Primitive
The Book of Bones

Stand-Alone Novels

Into the Woods
Arena of Souls
The Zombie-Driven Life
You Suck

Callsign: Queen (with Jeremy Robinson)
Destiny (with Sean Ellis)
Dark Rite (with Alan Baxter)
Primordial (with Alan Baxter- forthcoming)

David Wood writing as David Debord

The Absent Gods Trilogy
The Silver Serpent
Keeper of the Mists
The Gates of Iron

The Impostor Prince (with Ryan A. Span)

TREASURE OF THE DEAD

Maddock and Bones set off on their first treasure hunting adventure!

1715- Blown far off course, their treasure-laden ship sinking, a crew of Spanish sailors struggles ashore, only to encounter a horror out of their worst nightmares.

Dane Maddock and Bones Bonebrake have left the Navy SEALs and set out on a search for the legendary lost treasure fleet. The search takes them to Haiti, where they encounter the forces of a madman bent on finding the treasure in order to fund his maniacal experiments and help him seize the power he craves. But not all their foes are human. Mystery, history, and legend meet as Maddock and Bones scour ancient ruins, plumb the depths of the sea, and come face to face with pure evil in their quest for the *Treasure of the Dead.*

Praise for David Wood and the Dane Maddock Adventures!

"Dane and Bones.... Together they're unstoppable. Rip roaring action from start to finish. Wit and humor throughout. Just one question - how soon until the next one? Because I can't wait." -Graham Brown, author of *Shadows of the Midnight Sun*

"What an adventure! A great read that provides lots of action, and thoughtful insight as well, into strange realms that are sometimes best left uncxplored." -Paul Kemprecos, author of *Cool Blue Tomb* and the *NUMA Files*

"A page-turning yarn blending high action, Biblical speculation, ancient secrets, and nasty creatures. Indiana

Jones better watch his back!"–Jeremy Robinson, author of *SecondWorld*

"With the thoroughly enjoyable way Mr. Wood has mixed speculative history with our modern day pursuit of truth, he has created a story that thrills and makes one think beyond the boundaries of mere fiction and enter the world of 'why not'?" -David Lynn Golemon, Author of the *Event Group* series

"A twisty tale of adventure and intrigue that never lets up and never lets go!" -Robert Masello, author of *The Einstein Prophecy*

"Let there be no confusion: David Wood is the next Clive Cussler. Once you start reading, you won't be able to stop until the last mystery plays out in the final line."-Edward G. Talbot, author of *2012: The Fifth World*

"I like my thrillers with lots of explosions, global locations and a mystery where I learn something new. Wood delivers! Recommended as a fast paced, kick ass read."-J.F. Penn, author of *Desecration*

Prologue

1715, Caribbean Sea

Alonso Sanchez paced the deck of the *El Señor San Miguel.* He scanned the waters ahead of them, searching for signs of the other ships in their fleet. The captain's decision to leave Havana for Spain after taking on supplies had seemed to be a sound one, for the terrible storms in this part of the world known as hurricanes were not usually known to happen this early in the year. Yet here they were, barely two days out of port, and the weather had taken a severe turn for the worst, heavy rain pelting the ship's wooden decks, thunderclaps booming in the distance.

They had first lost sight of the fleet about half a day ago, when one of the smaller masts had snapped in the storm. Unable to fully control the ship, they had slipped off course. At the time it had seemed an event of little consequence. All of the fleet's dozen ships—eleven Spanish and one French—were heading for the same destination, after all. The *San Miguel's* crew would make repairs as soon as weather allowed and they would catch up. Sanchez had lost count of the times inclement weather had caused them to become separated from their sister ships. But those separations from the fleet were usually a few hours at most. To lose sight of eleven ships for half a day could mean only one thing: they had fallen irretrievably off course and were now lost. Separated. On their own.

This prospect sent a most uncomfortable chill coursing along Sanchez's spine. No fewer than half a dozen European nations had warships plying the seas looking for Spanish treasure ships, particularly those making the return voyage to Spain, which would be laden with gold, silver and untold jewels. Even when part of a fleet, they were a target worth pursuing. But a lone treasure ship, holds brimming over with riches such as the *San Miguel's* was now? She was a type of vessel known as a *carrack*—both lighter and faster than a galleon, but also relatively unarmed, meant to be escorted by a fleet, and if necessary, to flee.

Sanchez crossed himself against the terrifying notion. Like all Spanish sailors, he had heard tales of what fates befell Spanish seamen captured at sea, and none of them involved anything other than unyielding torture and eventual death. Many a man would throw himself into an angry tempest of a sea rather than be taken alive by an English ship, or even worse, rogue pirates.

Sanchez turned around and stared nervously into the gray soup that was the northern sky. If they turned around now they could get back to Havana, wait for the weather to clear and then join up with another friendly fleet returning to Europe. Sanchez knew he was but a lowly rank-and-file sailor, though; his opinion mattered not at all to the Crown and the captains to whom they entrusted their precious treasure fleet. He stood and watched as the *San Miguel* sailed on into the confusing gloom. He thought he could make out a mountainous landform in the distance, but he couldn't be sure with the swirling clouds and pelting rain.

Making matters worse, Sanchez flinched with a sudden flare-up of pain in his lower jaw. He'd been experiencing an agonizing toothache for the past several weeks, and the ship's doctor had continually promised to look at it without actually doing so. Sanchez decided to take his mind off of their problematic navigation by going to see him now. He worked his way along the deck, grabbing onto ropes here and masts there for support against the forceful elements, until he reached the entranceway to the rear belowdecks. He descended the ladder and held his breath against the stench of vomit from seasick sailors holed up against the weather.

The ship's doctor, one Cristobal D'Avila, kept a small private room that doubled as his quarters and office. Many times the crew had been reminded how fortunate they were to have an actual, trained physician on board as opposed to a barber who acted as one simply because he was in possession of cutting implements, as was often the case on many a ship. Yet, Sanchez reflected as he took in the line of men camped outside the doctor's door, this physician never seemed to be available to help. Sanchez brought his hand up to the outside of his mouth where the pain manifested.

"Who is he seeing?" he asked his fellow sailors who waited by the door.

One of the men, a youngster from Seville, Spain who sought treatment for fever, answered Sanchez. "He has been with the captain for some time now."

"What ails the captain?"

No sailor liked to hear his captain was anything less than one hundred percent. Especially when things had already gone south.

"Nothing anyone can tell. It seems more like they are having a meeting. I hear it might be to discuss—"

Suddenly they heard, and felt, the sound of wood grating over coral reef. It was a sensation sailors who ventured to this part of the New World had grown to fear with a vengeance. If they were lucky, the bottom of the hull would barely scrape over the reef and they would soon be on their way none the worse for wear. But as it happened the ship ground to a halt and Sanchez was thrown into a bulkhead, making it abundantly clear that this time they would not be so lucky.

"We've run aground!" one of the men shouted. He pounded on the door to the doctor's office. "Captain! We've run aground!"

"We've got water in here!" called a sailor from another part of the ship's hold.

"Captain? Doctor!" the men continued knocking on the door to no avail. Sanchez pulled a blunderbuss from a scabbard he wore around his waist, one he'd taken off a pirate he'd killed in close quarters battle, and wielded the long gun butt first. He looked to the door, then to his fellow sailors. They nodded in return. "Break it. If something happened in there, we need to know."

Sanchez backed up with the weapon. He was about to

ram the butt of it through the door when the ship canted violently to the port side. Unbelievably, water poured in from above them; a gaping hole in the starboard side of the hull was now exposed to huge breaking waves rolling over the foundering vessel. Two of the sailors ran out past Sanchez, heading for the main deck. One of the two remaining again pounded on the door and tried the knob, but after receiving no response, he, too, turned and fled for safety.

Sanchez also recognized that his life was not worth staying behind to raise the captain. For all he knew, their commander might not even be in there any longer. Holstering his blunderbuss, he high-stepped through the incoming water just as the ship rolled some more.

Any hope he harbored of the situation being improved by being out on deck was dashed the second he thrust his head into the open air. Although mid-afternoon, the sky was dark, making it difficult to see where exactly they had come to lie. Sailors' screams carried over the crashing of waves against the ship. Many men were washed off the vessel's tilted decks onto the razor sharp reef where they were shredded to pulp by oncoming seas before being swept away to drown. Sanchez was sure he was about to share their fate when a flash of cloud-to-ground lightning illuminated a shocking sight: trees, not far away. Land! They had not struck some oceanic shoal or shallow reef, but had come to an actual island.

Sanchez gripped some remaining rigging with his eyes fixed on the tree line he had seen, now in darkness once again. He dared not move his head for fear he would lose the position. He waited for one more thunderous wave to explode on the *San Miguel*, timing his exodus from the ruined vessel. He clutched the wet ropes, knowing that to let go now would mean being carried away to his death. He heard the cries of sailors who had either not managed to find something to hold onto or who had been washed away, regardless.

Rushing water cascaded over his body and then drained

off, leaving him still clinging to his precarious hold. He filtered out the screams of the dying in order to listen for another approaching wave. Unable to hear one coming, he leapt from his perch into the water. He was a poor swimmer and so exulted in the feel of the uneven reef beneath his feet. Clutching a loose piece of wood for support and to use as a shield from wayward debris, he began slogging his way toward the dark and mysterious shoreline.

He did not know what island this was, knew only his general location, somewhere in the Caribbean. Behind him, he could hear a few other sailors following in his soggy footsteps, shouting and calling to one another. Sanchez remained quiet for now, terrified that he would lose his fix on the tree line and end up walking to a watery grave.

The sea grew shallower as he made his way, and then it became apparent to Sanchez that others had made the shore before him. He could see people walking in front of the trees. They staggered, no doubt exhausted and injured from their trying ordeal, as was he. He headed for them, pleased that at least some of his shipmates had survived, that he would not face the trials and tribulations of this strange new land, no doubt populated by savages, alone.

"Hey! It's me, Alonso!" He stepped from the waves onto the coral shore and walked up the beach until dry sand caked his wet feet. "Carlos? Is that you?"

No one answered him. The wind must be carrying my voice away, Sanchez thought. He stepped closer to the trees, beyond which he could make out nothing but impenetrable darkness. One of the figures turned toward him and began to walk away from the trees, an ungainly ambling.

"Let me help." Sanchez ran to his shipmate's aid. He reached out for him to lend support, but his hand froze when a bolt of lightning cast the man's face in an otherworldly glow.

"My God, what happened to you?" Sanchez withdrew his hand, wondering if this man had some sort of communicable disease. But before he could arrive at an answer, the castaway swiped at Sanchez aggressively.

Sanchez reached for his blunderbuss only to pass a hand over an empty scabbard. The gun had been ripped away during his escape from the ship.

The assailant lunged at Sanchez, mouth open, eyes wide. His grimy fingers passed through the sailor's hair and Sanchez spun away from his attacker. He made up his mind right then that flight, rather than fight, was the preferable option here.

Sanchez dashed into the woods, outpacing his strange pursuer, but aware that other figures lurked in the shadows.

Chapter 1

Jacmel, Haiti

The priest sat alone in his church. David Abbe had performed a modest service that morning and then spent quiet time tidying up the place. A small but very old building, the weight of history lay on its two short rows of pews, altar, and simple lectern. An unadorned wooden cross hung on the wall. The decor was functional rather than ornate. The people served by this house of worship were poor, close to the earth, and required no ostentatious displays to feel close to their god.

Though he sometimes longed for a more prestigious appointment in a finer setting, there were some advantages to his current position, Abbe reflected. His current appointment required comparatively little of his time, given that his congregation was so small. This afforded him the luxury of regular rest and reflection, and permitted him time to pursue his other interests. He gazed up at his own podium, trying to see things as his parishioners did, to gain perspective. He had begun to imagine himself delivering a sermon, to let his thoughts drift, when he heard footsteps on the church stairs.

A visitor.

Taking a deep breath, Abbe rose and faced the door. The person who darkened the doorway was tall and slender. He looked as though he could be local, a Haitian black man, like Abbe himself, but the priest did not recognize him. Perhaps this visitor hailed from another village. He addressed the man in Haitian Creole, a French-based language with Portuguese, Spanish, and West African influences that reflected the nation's diverse history.

"Welcome to this house of God. You are free to sit." He motioned toward a nearby chair.

The newcomer entered the building but did not take a seat. "Father Abbe," he replied in English, "I come here not to pray, but to speak with you personally."

Abbe raised his eyebrows in surprise. This man knew him by name. "Oh? What about?" His best guess was that he wanted money, or perhaps the help of the church for some sort of community fund raiser or charitable act. Or perhaps personal counseling, though that was rare in a place where people were too busy surviving to reflect on things like whether or not they were happy. If it wasn't one of those three, he had absolutely no idea.

"I would like you to tell me about an exorcism performed by a priest, here in Jacmel."

"Oh, performed by whom? Father Paulin?" Paulin was a friend of Abbe's, the priest for the next parish over, and was known to do an exorcism now and again. Contrary to popular belief spawned by Hollywood horror movies, the practice as it was done in Haiti was fairly routine and sometimes little more than easing a tormented soul, a form of therapy, really.

"No, Father Abbe, this particular exorcism was performed in the year 1715." The visitor paused to let this sink in.

The hairs on Father Abbe's arms began to stand on end. He told himself to stay calm, that he was getting ahead of himself. He cleared his throat and said, "For historical matters, you would do well to consult the village librarian. I do believe the library is open today."

"Think hard, Father Abbe. 1715. Exorcism. Tell me what comes to mind."

The only sound while the two men made eye contact was that of a bird fluttering its wings high in the church's rafters. Something about the visitor, and not only his odd request, was putting Abbe extremely off balance.

The priest shook his head and held his hands up in a show of emptiness. "Nothing comes to mind, I'm afraid. As I suggested, the librarian might…"

The visitor held up a hand. "Please. There is no need to

waste both of our time, not to mention that of the librarian. I am aware of your research into lost treasures. Perhaps if you think about the exorcism in that context, we can enjoy an amicable conversation. If not..."

He let his words hang while watching the invisible noose tighten around Abbe's neck. *This man knows, somehow he knows...*But Abbe composed himself and maintained the lie.

"Yes, I have been conducting research for a historical book I'm writing, but I am aware of no connection to an exorcism during that time period, or any exorcism, for that matter."

The visitor's eyes narrowed slightly. "I will give you a moment to reconsider your answer. Think carefully."

Abbe did his best to feign indignation and exasperation. He exhaled heavily before saying, "This consultation will have to conclude, sir. I have other duties to attend, and repeating myself over and over is not productive."

The visitor stared at Abbe for a second, as if considering something, but then said, "I suppose we have no more business. I will be back when you've had time to contemplate."

"I've already told you…"

The man held up a big hand, palm facing outward. "Not the exorcism. Take time to reflect upon your own mortality."

He turned and walked out of the church without so much as a glance back, but something about the way the man spoke the words unnerved Abbe. The voice was very cold, brimming with a negative energy the priest was unable to place yet at the same time was unable to deny.

He waited for a couple of minutes to be sure the man had truly left, that he was not loitering outside the church, composing his thoughts only to return with a new angle of attack. When Abbe felt certain the visitor had departed the premises, he turned and strode to the front of the church. He climbed the short stairway to the elevated platform on which the podium was situated. A woven mat covered the platform behind the podium. He slid it aside, revealing a handle set into a cutout section of wood.

Looking up once at the doorway, Abbe lifted the wood panel out of the platform and set it aside. He reached into the space below the platform where he kept a few items that others need not know about. A loaded pistol. A knife. A small cache of emergency canned food and water. Abbe was a man of God but also a man who believed that God helped those who helped themselves. When he reached even further into the concealed space, past these contingency items, his fingers passed over a weathered, wooden cigar box.

He removed the box and opened its lid, rejoicing in the familiar, sweet smells, odors that lingered even though the box had not held cigars for many years. He carefully lifted a sheaf of brittle, yellowed papers from the container and eyed them with a mix of promise and trepidation. Words written in longhand filled the pages, some in Spanish, others in French.

Abbe read over some of them, not for the first time, his heart racing. He looked up at the empty doorway and a thought overtook his senses, slowly at first but gathering momentum by the second. The priest smiled as he tucked the box beneath his cassock and replaced the section of wood back into the platform. He needed to get these somewhere safe, and he knew just what to do with them.

Abbe stepped out of the church and into the warm, humid night air. Though still unnerved by the strange visitor early in the day, he took comfort in the fact that his research was on the way to somewhere safe, and the rest of the day had passed without incident. He locked the door, descended the short flight of wooden steps and began to walk the familiar quarter-mile or so to his residence. He had gone no more than a few steps when a ragged man with unkempt hair, threadbare clothes, and a gap-toothed leer, staggered toward him out of the bushes.

Abbe gave him a glance and frowned. Under a different

set of circumstances he would offer assistance, but tonight was not that night. "I am sorry, church is closed for the night. Come back in the morning there will be a simple breakfast and prayer." He was accustomed to helping those in need, but in Haiti, the poor were, as the scriptures said, always among him, and even the most faithful servant had to rest.

The man kept coming.

"Please, come back tomorrow and the church will see to your needs."

But still he approached. Abbe took a closer look at him now. Was the man in need of medical attention? There were no street lights in this part of the village, and so Abbe could make out little detail of the man. But something was definitely off about him—the way he said nothing, his odd movements. Abbe decided he could be in danger—the individual could be on drugs—so he speed-walked down the road. At the first intersection he reached he turned left ...

...only to be confronted with a similar, ambling figure.

At first Abbe questioned whether this could be the same man he had seen a block back—that he had somehow beaten him to this spot, even with his ragged gait. Were his eyes playing tricks on him? It had been a long day, after all. But then, as his eyesight adjusted to the low light, he realized that the clothes this person wore were different. Not the same man.

Yet he acted like the other man, stumbling, not speaking even though he had clearly seen Abbe. What kind of man said absolutely nothing to another when passing by on the street at night? Not a simple hello, hey, good evening....nothing to assure the other that he harbored no ill intentions. Very strange for the village.

And then another individual stepped onto the road out of the trees, and still another after him.

Abbe stopped in his tracks. This must be some kind of gang, doped up on God knows what. He would report it tomorrow to the police and offer his church's assistance. For right now, though, he needed to get out of here and back home safely. This way wasn't going to work, so he turned around to go back the way he came. He'd rather deal with a single one of these freaks than a whole gang of them.

But as soon as he faced the opposite direction he was stunned to see no fewer than four more of the figures coming his way.

"What is it you want?" he called to them, repeating himself as he spun in a circle. None of them answered, but all of them continued to close in on him. The figures now blocked the road in both directions, leaving the thick jungle on either side as his only option for escape.

He ran for it, more than willing to take his chances with the spiders and snakes and whichever of God's creatures lurked inside, but as he stepped off the road onto the wet, high grass that bordered the trees, two more of the men emerged from the forest, arms outstretched toward him.

Flabbergasted, Abbe spun around to bolt for the woods on the opposite side, but three more of them were upon him, hands tearing at his clothes, scratching and clawing at his exposed skin with long, dirty fingernails. He could hear and feel their ragged breathing, but even in the throes of their physicality they remained wordless, violence their only language.

"Please, I serve the Lord. Have mercy..."

But apparently these were not men of God, nor were they men of words, for just as they didn't use them, they didn't respond to them, either. The weight of his attackers pushed Abbe to the ground. Hands clutched him, nails dug into his skin. Hot breath assaulted his nostrils. His scream drowned in a gurgle of blood as teeth tore through his throat.

Chapter 2

Cherokee, North Carolina

Dane Maddock crinkled his nose as he passed through the cloud of blue smoke that greeted him as he entered Crazy Charlie's Cherokee Casino. He navigated the throng of gamblers bathed in the dull neon light of slot machines, sidestepping the scantily clad serving girls, bypassed the blackjack tables, and managed to reach the bar without anyone spilling a drink on him. That was a rarity in this place, where few customers stayed sober for long.

"It's about time." A beautiful young woman greeted him. She smiled at him and gave a wink.

As Maddock tried to pretend he wasn't staring at her perfect cheekbones, big brown eyes, glossy hair, and trim, athletic figure, he marveled that Angel Bonebrake shared DNA with his best friend, Bones.

"Sorry. Flight was delayed out of Atlanta. You know how it is."

Angel rolled her eyes at the mention of the Atlanta airport. She waved to the bartender, who hurried over to her. The gleam in his eyes said he was at her beck and call. Angel had that effect on men. That is, when she wasn't punching them in the throat or kneeing them in the groin as a professional mixed martial arts fighter.

"Dos Equis, right?"

Maddock had let his eyes drift to Angel's tight jeans and it took him a moment to realize she was talking to him. "That's right. I'm surprised you remembered."

Angel flashed a knowing smile. "I pay as much attention to you as you do to me. You know I'm a sucker for a blue-eyed blond."

Maddock wasn't sure what she meant by that, but a warm, uncomfortable feeling washed over him as she passed him a bottle of beer.

"To getting my brother straightened out." She raised her bottle.

"Cheers," Maddock said. The clink of glass on glass seemed to sharpen his focus, and he managed to dismiss thoughts of Angel. Those were thoughts that could get him into serious trouble. She was his friend's sister. Besides, Maddock had a girlfriend, albeit a long-distance one.

Angel took a long drink, sighed, and let out a loud belch. Beneath that flawless exterior, she was a Bonebrake through and through. "I need to warn you, it's bad."

"That's what you said when you called." Since leaving the SEALs several months before, Maddock had found the adjustment to civilian life difficult, and according to Angel, Bones was having an even harder time.

"I didn't tell you the worst of it. It's not just that he's been lying around drinking, but he's started roughing up the customers." She made a sweeping gesture that took in the entire casino floor.

"He *is* a bouncer," Maddock pointed out.

"But he's not a hit man for the mafia." Angel took another drink, appearing to consider her words. "His job is to de-escalate situations, and if necessary, to escort patrons from the premises. Call the cops if needed. But he's not doing that."

Maddock nodded. A quick scan of the casino revealed a customer base comprised largely of what Bones would consider rednecks—his least favorite social class.

"I imagine the John Deere caps get on his nerves."

Angel's laugh was as lovely as the rest of her, and Maddock forcefully redirected his thoughts to Bones as she continued.

"I wish that were the only problem. I don't want to say he's changed, Maddock, but he's like… I'll sound like a drama queen if I say he's like a caged animal, but it's something like that. He's got a skill set he can't really use in civilian life, and he has no outlet for all his bottled-up energy. I tried to get him to go to the gym with me but he says he only fights for real, not in a cage for money. He hasn't even gone climbing since he got out." She cast a reproving look at Maddock.

"I know. I've been meaning to get together with him, but frankly, I've had my own problems figuring things out." He took a swallow of his Dos Equis, savoring the cool drink as it sluiced down his throat, already irritated from all the smoke in the air.

"And you've been making trips to D.C., I gather?" Angel playfully punched his shoulder. "I hear you met a girl."

"I did." He took another drink so he wouldn't have to elaborate. Thinking about Melissa made having drinks with Angel feel almost like cheating.

"I did," Angel deadpanned in a dull voice. "I'm sure she appreciates how excited you are about your relationship."

Maddock managed a sheepish grin. "You know me. I'm all about the job."

"You and Bones are different in the particulars, but at heart, you two are a lot alike. You both need to loosen up and have some fun." She drained her bottle, slammed it on the counter, and belched again. "And you need a new purpose in life." She slid off her barstool and looked around. "My idiot brother's over by the roulette wheel. Let's go talk to him."

Even in an Armani suit and with hair that now hung down to his shoulders, Bones was recognizable by his sheer size. He towered over everyone else and customers gave him a wide berth. He stood, powerful arms folded across his chest, staring disapprovingly at a boisterous group of young men who appeared to be having a blast while losing prodigious amounts of money. His head snapped around and his eyes locked immediately on Maddock.

"Screw you, Maddock," Bones rumbled.

"He hasn't even said anything, you assclown."

"Screw you too, Angel."

Angel stepped forward, grabbed her brother by his bolo tie, and yanked his head down. "Bones, if you want to keep all those pretty teeth, you'd best remember that I'm a lady."

Bones guffawed and Maddock turned his head to hide his laughter.

Angel wasn't fooled. "You both suck, you know that?" She turned and stalked away.

Maddock found himself choosing between admiring her as she walked away and facing his angry friend. He chose the latter.

"What are you doing here?" Bones asked, only a little of the chill absent from his tone.

"I came to talk to you. I've got something cooking and I want you to go in on it with me."

Bones smirked. "If it's not a strip club, I'll pass. But you wouldn't do anything that interesting, would you? What is it?"

"Marine archaeology. I mean, treasure hunting," Maddock added. "You know, finding shipwrecks and gold?"

Bones stared down at him for a long moment and then shook his head. "No thanks."

"Come on, Bones. We did plenty of treasure hunting when we were in the service. This is a chance to do it again, and without people shooting at us."

"That was the fun part." Bones' countenance fell. He looked sadder than Maddock had ever seen him.

Just then, one of the young men at the roulette wheel threw up his hands and began shouting about "cheating Indians."

Bones closed the distance between them in two strides, grabbed the young man by the wrist, and spun him about.

"Are we going to have a problem?"

The young man winced as Bones squeezed his wrist. "No, sir," he squeaked.

Still maintaining his grip, Bones turned to the rest of the group. "Are we all going to have a good time or do we all need to take a walk?"

The frightened looks in their eyes and their stammered assurances that they were just there to gamble were all Bones needed. He released the young man, who immediately began rubbing his wrist.

"Walk with me, Maddock." Bones strode away, and Maddock had to double-time it to keep up with the six foot-five Cherokee. "I'm bored," Bones said to no one in particular. "There's nothing here to do, and my one friend disappeared on me."

Maddock sensed this wasn't the time to argue, so he kept his silence.

"But you know the real problem?" Bones continued. "The only thing I know how to do is kill people, and that's not a skill set anyone needs in civilian life. I invested years in the SEALs and now I'm useless."

"You're wrong," Maddock said. "You'd be great at treasure hunting. We'd be at sea again, diving all day, sitting on deck drinking beer at sunset, meeting girls in all the ports."

Bones laughed. "I'd be meeting girls. You'd be on the boat writing love letters to Melissa. How is she, by the way?'"

"She's good. But seriously, I want you to work with me."

"Treasure hunting sucks, Maddock. Reading maps, working a grid all freaking day long, hoping to get a hit on sonar. It's not for me."

"Hey, Bones! Who's your friend?" A curvy waitress sidled up to them and cast a predatory glance at Maddock.

"Don't bother," Bones said. "He's gay."

The girl laughed. "Yeah, right. Some of us are meeting up later if you two want to join?"

"He's leaving first thing in the morning." Bones inclined his head toward Maddock. "But I might give you a call."

The girl thrust out her lower lip, vowed to hunt Bones down if she didn't hear from him, and slinked away.

"I'm not leaving in the morning," Maddock said. "Matter of fact, I'm sticking around until you agree to at least give treasure hunting a try. Look, I know I haven't been a good friend. It took me a while to figure things out for myself. I'm still not sure I'm cut out to be a civilian, but at least I've got a direction. You could use one too."

"You shouldn't have talked me into leaving the SEALs," Bones said. "It was the only thing I was ever good at."

Maddock privately thought he hadn't convinced Bones of anything, but he knew that protest would fall on deaf ears. "You're selling yourself short, you know? You've got a lot more to offer than that."

Bones rounded on him. "Oh yeah? Like what?" Before Maddock could answer, he held up a big hand. "Never mind. I don't want to hear your Mister Rogers crap."

"Fine. How about we go climbing tomorrow?"

"I've got to work." Bones frowned and slowly scanned the room. "Dude, you wouldn't believe how many chicks are checking you out right now."

"I'm sure they're looking at you."

"Nope. You're something we never see in North Carolina—a white guy with all his teeth."

They shared a laugh, a genuine one, and Maddock sensed a lightening of the tension.

"You really need to get out of here before a gap-toothed woman in a tube top makes you her boy toy."

Maddock nodded. "How about my offer?"

Bones sighed. "I'll think about it."

Chapter 3

Jacmel, Haiti

They called him Odelin, and no one knew if that was his first or last name. No one cared, either, because he was the boss, at least as far as those here with him were concerned. They had heard him on occasion talking on the phone with someone he obviously had to answer to, but that was not their problem.

Odelin looked over at the remains of the priest he had visited earlier. His men wrangled the blood-soaked corpse into the panel van they'd parked in an alleyway here at the edge of the worst part of town. As soon as they had stowed the whole messy bundle inside, Odelin told the driver to wait and stepped inside the vehicle. He pulled on a pair of latex gloves and knelt before the mangled deceased. One of his men asked if he would like help searching the body, but Odelin refused. The matter was too sensitive and critical for that level of help. "I'll handle it. Just keep watch and alert me if anyone approaches by any means."

The man nodded and left him alone. Odelin proceeded to search Abbe's body, a disgusting task given the nature of his demise, but one that was wholly necessary.

Come on, preacher man, make this easy on us.

But a few minutes of thorough searching later and Odelin had nothing to show for it but a pair of bloody gloves. Frustrated, he stripped them off and tossed them unceremoniously onto the deceased before exiting the van.

He told his men to wait while he walked to the nearest dwelling, a dilapidated mobile home that happened to have electricity and running water, utilities that were not a given in this part of the world. Used as a low key safe house for his organization, Odelin detested the ramshackle place but found it to be an effective lair in which to lay low and get things done from time to time.

Once inside, he locked the door behind him. He cursed at the rats that scurried off at his sudden approach before making his way into the kitchen. For some reason this is where the phone was kept, something about it being the only accessible point where the illicit wiring job could be tapped into the mains. He opened a cabinet and took down the pushbutton landline telephone.

Odelin dialed from memory and when the other end picked up, he said without preamble, "He doesn't have it."

A pregnant pause ensued during which Odelin could sense his superior's disappointment.

"What steps are you taking?"

"I have my men searching the church and the priest's home as we speak. I will let you know the second they find anything."

"See that you do."

The words were direct enough, but Odelin recognized them for the threat they were and shivered as he replaced the handset in the cradle.

See that you do. He flashed on the times former associates of his had heard that same phrase and then failed to deliver. He watched a cockroach scurry up the wall and into a crack where the wall met the ceiling. He would be living like that, too, if this search didn't pan out—running for cover of darkness for the rest of his short-lived days.

He picked up the phone again and dialed a new number. He had already told his man to report in after the search had been completed, but that was when he had thought he would hit paydirt on Abbe's body. He had been all but certain the priest would not allow something so important to ever be out of his direct possession, especially after being confronted about it. But he had thought wrong.

It was time to find out how the other search was progressing.

Chapter 4

Cherokee, North Carolina

Maddock pulled in to the parking lot of the Cherokee Suites. He cut the engine of his '75 Bronco and took in the pitiful site—faded paint, sagging roof, cracked windows. He shook his head at Bones' living situation. This was no place for a seasoned and talented warrior of Bones' caliber. But his friend had to want to take steps, and that's why Maddock had come. His former comrade in arms hadn't been interested in his business proposition last night in the casino, but maybe now, after some time to reflect and calm down a bit, he would be open to reason.

He found the room number Angel had given him and knocked on the door. Hopefully Bones wouldn't be still in bed with one of his hookups. Something told Maddock his friend's mood was too dark lately for such frivolity. A few seconds came and went. Maddock knocked again.

"Unless you're a hooker, go away. I don't need to find Jesus and I don't need housekeeping."

Maddock smirked. "I'm sure it's a pigsty in there, Bones. Open up."

Maddock heard the thump of feet hitting the floor and stomping across the room. The door cracked and the Indian's face looked out at Maddock from behind his unkempt hair. "Get your own room, Maddock, they've got vacancies. You'll love it. These twin beds are like king size luxury mattresses compared to the barracks cots."

"Yeah, I remember your feet always used to hang off. How's the flea situation?"

"They don't eat too much."

"That's good. Can I come in for a few minutes?"

Bones undid the security chain and pulled the door open. He stood aside while Maddock entered, took in the gloomy, disheveled look of the place at a glance, and then opened the curtain. Bones closed the door and squinted at Maddock. "Too bright."

"Since I'm hoping you'll see that light, that works for me." Maddock took one of the two chairs at the little round table in front of the room's only window and turned one of them toward his friend.

"Sit. Hear me out."

"Is this about that treasure stuff you were blabbing about last night?"

"Yes. But I'm not just talking about it, Bones. I'm doing it. I already bought the boat and the equipment. Now I'm looking for a qualified partner, preferably one I've worked with before."

Bones said nothing, but Maddock took solace in the fact that he wasn't laughing yet. And he couldn't really blame him if he did. It was a common reaction Maddock got from a lot of people. *Treasure hunting, huh?* He could hear the doubt lurking in their voices, practically hear them saying, *Why don't you just get a real job?* None of them knew the first thing about treasure hunting, though, especially underwater treasure hunting. But Bones did, even if he acted like he didn't give a damn.

"What kind of boat you get?"

Maddock grinned. Finally he was getting somewhere. "You remember Marco Cosenza's boat?"

Recognition took hold over Bone's features. "The *Sea Foam*?"

Maddock smiled and nodded.

Bones looked incredulous. "That old scow?"

"One and the same." Maddock's thoughts flashed to a whirlwind adventure through and beneath the streets of Boston in search of Paul Revere's famous lanterns. The distant look in Bones' eyes told him his friend was doing the same.

"I've done a lot of work on her: overhauled the engine, new wiring, fresh bottom paint, retrofitted with state-of-the-art electronics..."

"So you're saying that ship is dependable and ready to go? Because I don't have a Sea Tow membership."

"She's more than up to the task, Bones. The question is...are you?"

Bones looked around the dingy room. "It'll be tough to give all this up, but..." His eyes lingered on a pile of empty beer cans on the floor, a hard liquor bottle among them. "But okay, I'm in."

Maddock gave him a hard stare. "Don't just *say* 'I'm in'. This is a serious commitment."

"Uh oh. I've heard that before."

"This is a partnership. I've already paid for the major stuff we'll need up front, but I'll need you to carry your financial weight going forward. Fuel, repairs, permits..."

"...hookers, blow. Priorities, Maddock."

"You'll need to give it your all. That's all I ask."

Bones stood, folded his arms, and frowned." It sounds workable, but there's one problem."

"And that is?"

"I'm not sure I can handle you being my boss."

"I won't be your boss, I'll be your partner. I can't do this myself. I spent everything I saved up while in the Navy on the boat and startup costs. Besides, when things get heavy, there's no one I can count on more than you. You've proven that time and again. That's why I'm here. There's no shortage of guys who would go in on this with me, but I know you can do it."

Bones moved to the window and stared through the dirt-smudged glass. "You've got a better opinion of me than I do."

"That wasn't always the case."

Bones chuckled. "Only because I thought you were an ass. Still do, just as not as big of one as before."

"That's the spirit. Seriously, though. You're at your best when you're under pressure or doing something that matters. This life isn't you."

"I said I'm in. No need to get all Sigmund Freud on me." He turned to face Maddock. "Lucky for you, I didn't drink all the money I earned in the service, and Charlie's treated me okay. I'll put in all I've got."

Maddock nodded. "Hopefully we can get some of the old gang in on it at least on a part-time basis. I gave Willis a call and he said he's game. Apparently, he hasn't been able to find steady work in Detroit."

"At least there'll be somebody else on the crew who doesn't have a stick up his butt." Bones smiled. "I know we're partners, but I'm going to go ahead and make an executive decision."

Maddock raised his eyebrows expectantly.

"I know which treasure I want to hunt for first."

Chapter 5

Atlantic Ocean

The prow of the *Sea Foam* sliced effortlessly through the choppy seas. Maddock manned the helm, alternating his gaze from the horizon to the chart plotter on the console in front of him. "Now leaving the Florida Keys behind, headed for Cuba, then on to Haiti." It felt good to be at sea. The cool, salty air filled his nostrils, eliciting memories of his youth growing up on the Florida coast. Even better, they weren't heading into danger on a military expedition.

Bones eyed the electronic map from his position in the co-pilot's seat. "How about we make a quick stop in Key West for the Duval Crawl, hit the Hog's Breath Saloon?"

Maddock frowned. "How about you stay focused, and if we score treasure we can hang out in the Keys on the way back."

"Man, we're gonna hold you to that, Maddock." The gruff voice of Willis Sanders walking into the cockpit cut in to the conversation. A fellow SEAL from their shared time in the Navy, Willis had joined Dane and Bones on more than one of their globe-trotting adventures. The tall, dark-skinned man nearly matched Bones in height and bulk. The top of his shaved head fell just a couple of inches short of Bones full height. He was currently in between assignments and agreed to join Maddock and Bones on this venture.

Maddock nodded and turned to his friends. "We've got some open water cruising ahead of us. Let me use some of the time to brief you on what I've learned so far about our target, the wreck of the *San Miguel*."

"I already know this crap. Do I have to listen?" Bones asked.

Maddock shot him a withering glance, and Willis and Bones gave him their attention as he began his summation.

"The San Miguel was part of the legendary 1715 Treasure Fleet. A Spanish Crown flotilla consisting of a dozen ships, all but one of them were lost in a storm—a hurricane, probably—on the east coast of Florida, near present day Vero Beach."

Maddock looked over from the wheel. His audience showed no signs of boredom yet, so he continued. "The one ship thought to escape the storm, the *San Miguel*, has never been found."

"Spill the beans, Maddock, what were they carrying?" Willis wanted to know.

"Silver and gold. Lots of it," Bones answered.

Maddock nodded. "Some treasure from this fleet has already been found. In fact, every now and then a coin, like a silver *real*—with the bust of the king on one side and the Crown's shield on the other— will wash up on the beach in Florida today."

Bones made a show of looking around the cramped quarters of the vessel, the open sea beyond. "You mean we could just lay around on the beach and wait for these things to wash up with a drink in our hand, watching the babes go by?"

Maddock smiled. "I'm hoping to speed things up by taking a more proactive approach. So back to the *San Miguel*...people have searched for her, but to date no trace of her has ever been found."

Willis looked puzzled. "So what do we have to go on that no one else does?"

Bones answered him with a sly grin. "Fabiola Baptiste. You remember her?"

Willis laughed. "Fabi Babi?"

Maddock looked away from the wheel long enough to say, "I dare you to call her that to her face."

Fabiola had been in the Navy as a database programmer during the three SEALs' tenure

"Word is, Bones is the one who said things to her face, ain't that right? She's your ex?"

"She's not an ex, she's an occasional."

"Damn, that's cold. So what's she got to do with all this?"

Maddock made a slight adjustment to the boat's course, and then steered the conversation back on track as well. "She lives in Miami," he said, jerking a thumb behind them, "but she's in Haiti now because she has relatives there. She contacted Romeo, here, because she received interesting information from a priest in Haiti, one who happens to be her cousin."

Skepticism painted Willis' face. "Why don't we just deal with the priest directly?" He turned to Bones. "No offense, Fabi's great and all, but let's cut out the middlewoman, know what I'm saying? Loose lips sink ships and all that."

Bones shook his head. "We can't contact the priest, David Abbe, because he's dead."

Willis cocked his head. "You try some voodoo stuff? It is Haiti, after all."

Maddock addressed him with a stern look. "He was murdered a week ago. It was ugly. Vicious."

Willis lowered his gaze. "You know I wouldn't joke like that in front of Fabi."

Maddock continued. "Here's what we do know: She received some information from her cousin, the Haitian priest, which frightened and confused her to the point where she called Bones for advice."

Willis chuckled. "Damn. She must have been scared all right. Who in their right mind calls Bones for advice?"

"Screw you, Willis. Fabi thinks she's in danger because of some information that came into her hands."

Willis threw up his hands. "You guys keep talking about 'some information'. What information?"

Bones leveled his gaze at Willis. "About the location of the wreck of the *San Miguel*."

Chapter 6

Petit-Trou-de-Nippes, Haiti

The scene was like something out of a postcard. Sugary sand beach lined with palms, one of them leaning way out over the turquoise, sun-dappled water. No tourist crowds. But just out of sight beyond the natural beauty lay a colder reality to the island, a poor community, many of whom struggled to get by on a daily basis. Amidst this contradiction in terms sat the *Sea Foam*, lying at anchor not far off the beach.

Maddock, Bones and Willis rode the *Sea Foam*'s dinghy to the beach in order to meet Fabi Baptiste. They found her waiting for them, as promised, at a small outdoor cafe on the side of the road fronting the beach. It was a local place, not a tourist establishment, not that there was a whole lot of tourism in Haiti compared to other Caribbean islands.

African and French on her father's side, Italian on her mother's side, Fabi had warm beige skin, hazel eyes, and full lips. She wore her hair in loose, shoulder length coils that bounced when she turned her head at the sound of Maddock's voice.

Bones greeted her first, giving her a big hug while Wills and Maddock exchanged knowing glances. When Bones released her, she eyed his companions. "Dane Maddock and Willis Sanders! Good to see you two alive and in one piece after all the crazy stunts you guys pulled in the SEALs."

Maddock and Willis also gave Fabi a hug, though not as long or close as the one from Bones.

"Damn, girl," Willis said. "You still working out?"

Fabi punched him in the shoulder, hard enough to make him wince. "What do you think?" She led them to a table in the "inside" area of the cafe, which was really just a shady nook under a section of corrugated sheet metal and surrounding banana palms. Plastic chairs were pulled up to a wooden picnic table on a dirt floor.

The three of them took seats and a Haitian woman took their orders, speaking in Creole. Maddock picked out several words in French, but that was all. She deposited a cold bottle of Prestige beer in front of each of them, and then left them alone. Fabi took a pull of her beer and then smiled at Maddock and Bones in turn.

"So, how's life on the outside treating you so far?"

None of the three men said anything, each waiting for one of the others to speak.

"That good, huh?" Fabi said.

"Well, we're here, so that's pretty cool," Bones said, looking around at the simple shack and the wall of jungle across the road.

"We just got our new treasure hunting venture off the ground." Maddock looked around and lowered his voice. He didn't see anyone else except for the woman who took their orders, but as a former SEAL, operational caution was bred into him. "And Bones put us on the trail of the 1715 fleet, the *San Miguel* in particular."

"What about you? What've you been up to?" Bones asked before taking a swig from his beverage.

"I've been volunteering at a health clinic here in Petit-Trou-de-Nippes."

"Sorry, there's no way I can get on board with petite nips." Bones grinned while Maddock looked around, hoping no one had overheard that, of all things they had to discuss.

Fabi rolled her eyes. "It translates to 'little hole of Nippes' and refers to the fact that the community grew up around a small harbor near the Nippes River that was deep enough for ships to anchor."

Bones grimaced. "Turns out petite nips was more interesting after all."

Fabi slapped Bones on the arm before continuing. "But listen. This is about my cousin, David. He's the reason I reached out to you, and unfortunately for me the news is not good." She hung her head in a moment of silence, then went on.

"He was a priest?" Maddock prompted.

Fabi nodded. "Someone found his body in the jungle not far from his church. It had been mutilated by animals, making it hard to tell what exactly happened to him."

"I'm sorry, Fabi." Bones held her while Maddock also expressed his condolences.

Fabi wiped her eyes and then continued. "David was a priest, yes, but he was a treasure hunter at heart."

She could read the looks in the men's eyes, looks that said, *How serious was he?* Lots of people daydreamed about finding lost treasure, maybe even read books or pored over maps and charts, armchair salvors. But those who actually ventured out into the ocean to look for it were few and far between. And what's more, both ex-SEALs realized, those who successfully recovered treasure in the ocean were even fewer still. The research needed to be solid, the execution highly competent, and then of course, that fickle mistress, Lady Luck, needed to make an appearance at least once.

But Fabi remained unfazed. "Take a look at this. He sent me a package shortly before he died." She set a simple bag on the table, looked up toward the entrance of the cafe once, and then removed from it a wooden cigar box.

Bones' face lit up. "Hey, all right. I hear they make fantastic cigars down here. Maybe not quite as good as the Cubans, but damn good, right? Can we light up in here?"

Fabi pulled some papers out of the box and smoothed them out on the table. "Sorry, Bones. Maybe if you're a good boy I'll see if I can find you a cigar later." She winked at him and Bones raised his eyebrows at Maddock, who leaned in closer to the papers.

"What do you have here?"

Her brow creased with concern. "This one here is a recent note from David saying he thinks someone is after the contents of the box and that they are dangerous. Looks like he was right. And he says what's in the box is very valuable."

Maddock stared at the old papers on the table, the

weathered box. "Why did your cousin send the box to you?"

Fabi sighed before looking up from the note. "David is...was... a gentle soul. Not much of a fighter. He knows I'm ex-Navy, knows I can take of myself, that I have a reputation for being a tough kid back in the day. And besides that, he trusts me. I'm family, I'm blood."

"So what's so valuable about what's in the box?" Maddock pressed.

Fabi glanced down at the yellowed papers. "I don't know the whole story, but I'm positive there's something in these documents that will lead us to treasure."

The gleam in Maddock's eyes was undeniable, but he forced himself to stay focused on the details at hand. But it was Bones who Fabi turned to next.

"You used to tell me about your experiences hunting for underwater treasures with Maddock, so when I thought about who to call, you were at the top of my list."

Maddock gave Bones a glance. "You do realize those were classified missions, right?"

The big Indian eyed Fabi. "All bets are off when trying to impress a beautiful girl."

Maddock shrugged, also looking to Fabi. "So did that work?"

It was her turn to smile. "Once or twice."

Maddock eyed the papers on the table. "I think we can help you with this."

Chapter 7

Jacmel, Haiti

Odelin swore as he paced within the narrow confines of the office at the back of the church. He and his men had torn the place apart, top to bottom. His hopes had risen when they discovered a secret compartment in the floor chancel area behind the pulpit, but inside were only a pistol and some general survival items. He thought it likely that what he sought was once in that hiding place, but for now his hopes had been dashed.

Making matters worse, he had just received word from one of his men that the search of Abbe's home had been completed and that effort, too, had produced no fruit. Odelin now had the most unenviable task indeed of reporting these developments to his boss. He dialed the desk phone in the church office and waited with the receiver to his ear. His superior came on the line and Odelin relayed the bad news.

His boss gave a sigh of exasperation. *"How certain are you that this record even exists, or still exists?"*

"One hundred percent certain. There can be no doubt. I have come across references to odd tales told by a priest long ago who died here while serving the church. The priest was never specific, but he referenced his journal and the ramblings of a sailor who confessed to him during an exorcism."

A pause ensued during which his boss seemed to digest this information. While he waited, he eyed the old personal computer on the well-worn desk. His eyes traced the dial-up modem cable from the phone jack to the PC. Then his boss was back on the line.

"Well then, what could Abbe have done with these documents if they were not on his person, nor in his home or place of work?"

"At this point I am considering many possibilities." Odelin wished he could give a better answer, but that was all he knew at this point.

"Do you think he might have turned them over to someone else, someone he trusted?"

Odelin sat down in front of the computer and saw that it was already powered on. He woke it from sleep mode and examined a few of the files on the system.

"Odelin, are you listening?" The tone was sharp. Odelin had become absorbed in looking at Abbe's files and forgotten that a response was required.

"Yes. One moment please, I may have found something interesting on Abbe's computer."

"Hurry up."

Odelin frowned as he found Abbe's internet email account and saw that it required a login and password. "One minute..." He riffled through the files in the largest desk drawer and found nothing, but as he replaced them, he noticed a tiny address book. Inside the front cover he found two words written in all lowercase: *david1984* and *c@1vary*.

"Calvary," he whispered. "What better password for a priest?"

"What's that?"

"Just another minute," he said. He typed in the two words. Success! "I'm in the account. Let's see what we've got here..."

Odelin scanned the list of email subjects, looking for anything that might tip them off to the contents having to do with the missing documents. He didn't know exactly what he expected to find, but after scrolling through a lot of them he didn't see anything that triggered recognition.

"Odelin? Is all of that keyboard tapping I'm hearing bearing fruit?"

He shifted from reading the subjects to looking at the sender and dates of the messages. He saw a number of emails from a Fabi Baptiste, recently received. He clicked on the SENT folder. There it was! He smiled.

"I've found exactly what we're looking for!"

Chapter 8

Petit-Trou-de-Nippes, Haiti

Maddock, Bones and Willis sat at a table with Fabi in the home of one of her relatives, an uncle who was out of town on business. The residence was a nice one, not a shack, and featured modern amenities including electricity, running water and contemporary furniture.

Maddock considered the documents from Abbe's cigar box which they had organized on the table, by date where possible, by similar paper type, and by language. All were old and appeared to have been cobbled together from different sources, perhaps torn from journals or logs of some kind.

"I think we're going to need Fabi to do the lion's share of the translation here, but I'm passable at reading French, so I'll take a shot at some of these." He indicated a stack of yellowed papers written in flowery longhand.

"I can deal with some Espa*ñ*ol," Bones said, reaching for a document written in Spanish.

Willis, who appeared bored by this process, agreed to take down a few notes when something meaningful was translated. "Let's just get this done. I signed up for treasure hunting, not paperwork."

The group worked for a time in silence, poring over the various documents. After a while Maddock summed up what they were thinking.

"It's difficult to see how these are connected, but from what I can tell so far, they reference different places on the island." He turned to Fabi. "You make anything of it yet?"

She furrowed her brow and slowly lifted one of the papers from the table. "Listen to this. It's an entry torn from a priest's journal, 1715." She squinted as she translated aloud in English:

The service of four sailors was required to hold the tormented sailor down. Possessed of inhuman strength, he could not be said to be of right mind, speaking as he was in odd tongues of living dead men and evil spirits unleashed into our dominion. In his cell in the old French fort, he had summoned extraordinary patience and will to carve strange things into the stone walls, symbols beyond our understanding should they contain meaning at all. My primary intention was to exorcise the spirits from his body responsible for his lunacy, but between my ministrations he exhibited moments of lucidity during which I could not help but take note of his fantastic tale.

The sailor recounted having been on a barrack that was part of a Spanish Crown treasure fleet of monumental value. Untimely storms separated the fleet, sank it and drove his ship far off course. They lost a mizzen mast and then a main and sailed blindly until they ended up on a reef somewhere off the shores of Hispaniola. He insists the storm was a punishment from God for the Spaniards' greed and for stealing from the native savages. Despite this punishment, he claims God also sent demons to punish any who survived the storm, and that these demons now guard the treasure fiercely and without prejudice.

Despite being in the throes of madness and the fantastical elements of his tale notwithstanding, I am compelled to think that the treasure of which this sailor speaks is as true as the word of God.

Fabi looked up from the faded page, eyes wide.

Willis underlined something he wrote on his notepad with a flourish. "'Priest says treasure is the real deal.' Just in case we forget what that said." He nodded to the document.

"Thanks, Willis." Maddock rolled his eyes. "Let's try to put this all together into something meaningful. Besides the passage Fabi just read, we know there are other entries that make mention of different points around the island. We also know for a fact that at least some of these entries are dated *after* that passage. That tells me that maybe this priest was going around the island, conducting his own hunt for a treasure he believed to be real."

"So we need to figure out what some of those places are." Bones eyed the mess of papers on the table dubiously.

Maddock went on. "Right, but we already have at least one solid clue from the page we just heard: he mentions an 'old French fort' where the sailor was kept prisoner."

"If it was old then, in 1715," Willis said, "it must be awful old now."

Maddock looked to Fabi. "Any old forts on this island?"

She nodded. "Many. But I have an idea where to start. Look at this."

She turned one of the papers around so the others could see. "The priest has written Saint Louis de Sud in the margin. I know there's an old fort there. I think we should check it out."

"Is it far?" Bones asked.

"It's not exactly close. On the plus side, it's on the Haiti side of the island of Hispaniola, which today, I'm sure you're aware, is shared with the country of Dominican Republic."

"But back in 1715 it was all known as Hispaniola," Maddock clarified.

Fabi nodded. "That's correct. Having to search on the Dominican side of the island would involve added complications."

"Then let's cross our fingers that this priest was on this side of the island." Willis actually crossed his fingers and held them up, but Fabi's face was downcast.

"What's wrong?" Willis asked. He looked at his fingers. "This some kind of taboo gesture in Haiti or something?"

She shook her head. "No, it's just that I haven't had the best luck with priests lately."

Chapter 9

Saint Louis de Sud, Haiti

They rode the dinghy up to the rickety dock and cut the engine. They secured their craft and climbed out, Bones going first to make sure the dock was sound. He tested the boards, then bounced on the balls of his feet a few times before giving them the thumbs-up.

"It'll hold me, so Maddock and Fabi should be good to go. Willis looks like he's been eating too much pizza lately, so he can go last."

Willis shook his head and gestured for the others to lead the way.

"Fort Des Oliviers is up this way and to the right," Fabi directed. They walked at a leisurely pace through the town, passing locals and tourists alike strolling on the sidewalks. Before long they found a sign to the fort. Maddock followed it until they spotted a crumbling stone facade on the edge of the Caribbean.

The four explorers approached the ruins. Stone walls, crumbling in spots, surrounded a flat, grassy area on which rusty cannons were spaced at regular intervals. Bones looked around. It wasn't exactly crowded, but a few people looked around or snapped photos.

Maddock stood still for a few moments and surveyed the scene. "I don't see anywhere up top that looks like somewhere a prisoner would be held. Is there a below ground section?"

"I haven't been here before so I'm not familiar with it myself," Fabi admitted. Some of the forts on the island do have subterranean chambers, but I don't know if this one does."

"Let's have a look." Bones took off toward the main grounds. The others fell into step behind him. As they walked they passed tourists having a look around, but the fact that many people had been here over the years, decades and centuries didn't dampen their spirits. Maddock and Bones knew from experience that simply because a place had lots of traffic, even heavy traffic, over time, did not mean that its secrets had been divulged.

They walked to the crumbling structure, had a look through one broken section to the coral beach just outside, then began to move along the perimeter wall, which was itself nothing noteworthy. They came to a junction between two walls where a gap between them left an opening in the earth. A stone stairway led down. Maddock suggested that they check it out, as the rest of the ground level appeared, at first glance, anyway, to be much the same as they had already seen.

Voices echoed below them down wherever the steps led, so Maddock knew this wasn't some secret passage, but it would help to get the lay of the land, so to speak. And who knew, he thought, producing a pocket flashlight, perhaps they could find something others had overlooked? They were, after all, looking for something specific as opposed to simply wandering around for the general experience.

Maddock stopped on the steps to closely examine the composition of the walls; as expected, they were fashioned of the same stone used on the fort's ground level. Bones passed Maddock and was the first to reach the bottom.

"One way up ahead." Bones waved an arm and started down a level corridor that left precious little clearance for his head. Willis and Fabi fell into step behind him and Maddock brought up the rear, pausing occasionally to examine a portion of floor, wall or ceiling with his mini-torch. After a hundred feet or so the passage jogged right.

Fabi's voice echoed off the walls. "So far it appears to be mirroring the same pattern as the wall above ground." The group continued along the passageway, which offered no branches or forks. At one point they had to squeeze by a couple standing in one spot fussing with a digital camera. Then they saw a flood of sunlight from above and came to what would be a dead end were it not for another stone staircase leading up.

Maddock scrutinized the walls and floor carefully before admitting that he saw nothing promising here, and then the group ascended the steps. They emerged back on the grassy quad area inside the perimeter walls.

"That was fun. Now what?" Willis wanted to know.

Maddock studied the grass area, nodding toward it. "With all this space here, you'd think there could be something underneath it, but from what we just saw the only digging they did here was on the perimeter tunnels."

Fabi nodded and pointed to a couple of toppled rock slabs here and there on the grass. "It looks like there may once have been structures on the quad area, but they were above ground only."

"It doesn't seem like we're missing anything here," Maddock concurred. Fabi pointed to a local man wearing a uniform of some sort with a lanyard and ID card around his neck. "He's a tour guide. Maybe he can fill in some blanks for us, make sure we haven't overlooked anything." She registered the nervous looks from the three ex-SEALs and then hastily added, "Without letting on what we're looking for, of course."

Maddock nodded and the four of them sauntered over to the guide, as if they were a casual group out for a lazy day trip. When they reached him, he was standing next to the perimeter wall with his hands behind his back, making himself available for questions but currently not helping anyone. They opted to let Fabi do the talking for them. She spoke to the guide in Creole, and he replied in the same.

"Good morning, sir. We're wondering if you can tell us a little about a story we've heard connected to an old fort somewhere on Hispaniola. We thought it might be this one, but we're not sure."

The guide prompted her to tell him the story and so she relayed a simplified version of a stark raving mad sailor held prisoner in a fort. After listening attentively, the guide replied.

"To my knowledge, Fort Des Oliviers is not associated with any such prisoner. It was used more as a defensible installation against approaching ships." He pointed out to the sea visible beyond the perimeter walls. "It featured heavy arms, lots of cannons, but was not used for holding prisoners."

Fabi's face fell upon hearing this, although Maddock and his fellow ex-SEALs remained impassive. The guide, seeming to sense Fabi's disappointment, added, "But you might pay a visit to Fort des Anglais, on the little island out in the bay." He pointed across the water, although the island could not be seen from their vantage point. "I believe that, due to its remote location, some prisoners were kept there, though I do not know about the sailor of which you speak."

Fabi thanked the guide and they ambled away as a group, not wanting to appear so eager as to bolt right off to the other fort. When they were some distance away from the man, Maddock said to the others, "Let's check it out."

Chapter 10

Off the coast of Saint Louis de Sud

The *Sea Foam* settled back into the water as Maddock eased back on the throttle. Willis occupied the co-pilot seat while Fabi and Bones caught up on old times on the rear deck. Maddock had decided it was worth making the drive back to Petit-Trou-de-Nippes in order to take their own boat to the island instead of looking for a rental, which would raise their profile, not necessarily a desirable thing to do when looking for treasure in this part of the world.

The island loomed before them, a forbidding hunk of rock overgrown with vegetation in the middle of a deep bay. Maddock eyed the boat's depth finder cautiously. They didn't need to run aground while hunting for treasure clues, but plenty of water lay beneath the hull even though they were close to shore. He gave the order as captain for Willis to drop anchor and Bones and Fabi to ready the dinghy. He expressed concern about leaving the boat unattended but Fabi said they should be okay for a while this far out in the bay.

Satisfied the *Sea Foam* was securely anchored, Maddock took in the weather. It was still warm out with some sun, but the sky had darkened in the southern quarter and a stiff breeze had cropped up, conjuring ocean swells. Still, Maddock didn't see a problem with the situation and so the four of them took off in the dinghy for the beach.

They got an even better look at the island as they drew near. Like a massive hunk of rock, its greenery-shrouded form jutted straight up from the sea. A narrow ring of flat beach and land surrounded it like a skirt. Maddock followed the island's perimeter until they reached a wide expanse of flat land with a few simple buildings visible, and in the distance, a stone facade.

Maddock pointed to a suitable spot on the beach to land the boat. He gunned the throttle and then Willis tilted up the outboard as the dinghy coasted up onto the sand with a grating hiss. They all got out and the men hauled the boat up high and dry onto the beach while Fabi scoped out their surroundings. She located a crushed coral path leading through some trees into the island's interior, and the group made their way along it, Maddock in front. They hadn't been walking for long when they heard a rustling of foliage to their right and above.

Maddock's hand moved instinctively to a machete he wore on his belt. Less than a second later, no fewer than six monkeys dropped out of the trees onto Willis and Bones. They were small, but strong for their size and moved with blinding speed. Willis was a blur of flailing arms as he flung the pint-sized primates from his body. Bones had a tenacious animal wrapped around his neck, which he tried to pry loose with one hand while batting two more off his head with his other.

The monkeys screeched and chattered while Maddock pulled one of them off Bones and flung it into the foliage. He repeated the process for Willis, and meanwhile Bones had stripped himself of his other two diminutive attackers. They ran the last monkey off and took stock of the damage.

"What the heck was that?" Bones wondered aloud. "Monkeys hating on us?"

"Wasn't too bad," Willis said, feeling along a scratch on his arm.

"Oh yeah? You got a bloody nose," Maddock pointed out.

Surprised, Willis touched his fingers to his nose and his eyes widened when they came away red. He pulled a bandana from a pocket and used it to wipe off the blood.

Fabi, meanwhile, had said nothing, but still stared after the monkeys retreating into the brush.

Bones followed her gaze. "You didn't tell me Haiti was full of killer monkeys."

She returned a puzzled look. "That's just the thing.

There are no monkeys in Haiti."

Willis snorted. "Man, tell that to those chumps who jumped us. What'd they want, anyway? I ain't got no bananas on me."

"There used to be monkeys here," Fabi went on. "And those..." She trailed off, evidently in deep thought.

"What about them?" Maddock prompted.

"They're a species known as the Hispaniola monkey."

"Oh, so there are monkeys on this island," Maddock said. "Or at least on the Dominican side. Is that where they're usually found?"

Fabi shook her head. "Not anymore. The Hispaniola monkey is thought to have gone extinct sometime in the 1500s."

Maddock shook his head as a thunderclap sounded somewhere in the distance. "Strange. Listen, is everybody okay?" They all nodded. "We should get moving, then."

They set out once again on the trail, hiking through the forest, now much more cautious about every sound they heard. The trees thinned on either side of them as they walked, until stone ruins were visible through the greenery on their right. They followed the path until it opened up onto a flat area where a stone fort crumbled from centuries of exposure to the elements. The four of them stood and took it in, marveling at the palpable history sitting out in the open. Fabi was the first to give voice to their thoughts.

"It doesn't look much different than Fort Des Oliviers, but this one is visited much more rarely."

Bones nodded. "I don't see or hear anybody."

"Just monkeys." Willis gave an uneasy grin while he picked at a deep scratch on his arm.

The first drops of rain from the storm Maddock had cautioned them about began to wet the ground. He waved them deeper into the old fort. "Let's do our recon and get back to the main island."

He received no arguments, and this time the four of them fanned out to cover more ground more quickly. This fort also featured a perimeter wall, crumbling in spots, but it had more structures than the previous fort. It took some time to search through these, but working separately they managed to get it done before long. The four of them reconvened in the center of the fort's open space area, each reporting that they had not discovered any spaces that likely would have been used to hold prisoners.

Dejected, and with the rain now starting to pour in earnest, Maddock signaled they should head back to the boat. They began walking through the fort's interior space. They had almost reached the point where they had entered when Fabi detoured a short distance to examine a spire-like construction. A stone column of sorts, it didn't appear to be a structure that could be entered, but she approached it nonetheless.

Maddock watched her near the spire. "See something interesting?"

"Not sure. It looks like…"

Suddenly the ground buckled beneath Fabi's feet and only her head and arms were left above ground, her hands gripping and clawing the earth.

"Fabi!" Maddock raced toward her, Bones and Willis close behind.

The rain intensified, now splattering Fabi's face with mud as she struggled to stay above ground. Maddock reached her, going into a forward, face-first slide as he watched her start to slip into some kind of crevice that had opened up. He extended both hands as he sought her grip. Their fingers touched for a second but not closely enough to establish a good grip.

Fabi disappeared into a subterranean space. Maddock, and now Bones, peered into the hole. They could just see her oval face down there, looking up at them. "I'm okay!"

"You sure?" Bones called back.

"Yes, nothing broken. You guys should come down. Drop's not too far, especially for you SEALs. This isn't a sinkhole, it's some kind of chamber. There's a lot of stone work down here, and it looks like I'm in a passage that could lead somewhere."

Maddock eyed Bones and Willis. "Got a rope? We'll need one to get back up." They shook their heads but then Willis spoke up.

"You two go ahead. I'll go back to the beach to grab the line off the dinghy, then I'll rig it up here and meet you down there."

Maddock nodded and he lowered himself into the hole until only his head and arms were above ground, as with Fabi. "Am I clear?" he called down to her.

"You're good. Maybe an eight foot drop onto flat stone. Go for it."

Maddock let go and landed with a grunt on flexed knees.

"Clear the landing zone." Bones let gravity take him down to Fabi and Maddock.

Willis' face appeared in the hole. "You guys good?"

"We're okay down here, Willis." Maddock gave him a thumbs up.

"Be back with the rope." He disappeared from sight and they heard his footsteps trammeling the ground as he left the fort.

Chapter 11

Fabi walked away from Maddock and Bones and they followed her down a stony corridor until it widened into a chamber. "This way looks like it opens up into a room." Here, the darkness was complete, and Maddock produced his flashlight to cast its halogen glow on the hewn walls.

Immediately they could see a multitude of unnatural shapes. Fabi pointed at a series of strange contraptions, made of iron and blackened wood.

"These look like fun." Bones winked at Fabi and held up a set of manacles attached to chains that were embedded in the stone wall.

"This looks more your speed, Bones." She went to a wooden wheel set up on a support stand.

"Not sure I want to know what that's for," Bones said, "but judging by the rest of this stuff, it doesn't look fun. Check this out." He ran his fingers lightly over a set of rusty spikes contained inside a coffin-like container shaped roughly like an adult human.

"That's the iron maiden." Maddock aimed his light beam on the medieval torture device.

"Classic stockade here." Fabi pointed to a hinged wooden board with cutouts for head and hands.

There were a plethora of other intimidating instruments but Maddock called a halt to the show and tell. "I think we can safely say this is a place where prisoners were kept."

Fabi concurred. "This stuff is old enough to be from the 1700s, and it certainly fits with a prison or holding cell of some kind from that period."

"Let's look around some more, see what else is down here. It'd be good to know if this passage leads somewhere else in the fort, or if Fabi literally fell into some luck by having the ground drop out from under her."

Maddock took a few flash photos of the torture devices

and the trio moved through the room into the passage, which continued on the other side. As he played his light about the walls here, he began to call the structural integrity of the underground space into question. They reached one section where the ceiling was lower than the rest of the corridor, and Bones in particular had to stoop to make it past.

He squeaked by and then the tunnel-like passage veered off to the right, narrowing as it did so. Maddock led the way with his light. As soon as they had all rounded the turn, Bones said, "Look out!" He dove into Fabi, pushing her out of the way of a chunk of rock that broke loose from the right-side wall near where it joined the ceiling. Both of them ended up lying on the floor, having just cleared the falling hazard.

Fabi turned around to see the pile of stone on the floor and Bones' black hair streaked with dust. "Honestly, Bones, I never took you for the type of man to push a lady around!"

"No, but I am known to get horizontal with a babe from time to time." Bones winked.

Maddock was all business, pushing ahead as soon as it was clear no one was hurt. Bones and Fabi moved along behind them, and before long they emerged into another room, this one more square, although still imperfectly shaped. Set into the four corners of this room were four jail cells, iron bars extending from floor to ceiling around each corner. A door was set into each, but they were all swung open as if abandoned in a hurry sometime long ago.

"Holding cells!" Maddock approached one and gripped the iron bars. "Still pretty solid."

Each of them went to a cell and began to inspect them. After a couple of minutes, Fabi said she might have found something. "Need some light over here."

Bones had also produced a flashlight and was first to join her in the small cell. Fabi traced her fingertips over a series of engravings in the cell wall.

"Random scribblings of a bored prisoner or something exciting?" Bones squinted as he tried to make sense of the carvings.

"It's writing." Fabi sounded less than certain. Maddock joined them in the now crowded cell, and he took snapshots of the inscriptions while Fabi continued her assessment.

"I'm pretty sure this is Spanish, but it seems a little like gibberish."

Bones looked around and shook his head. "I'd go crazy too if I were stuck in here for any length of time."

"You already are crazy, Bones," Fabi quipped.

"Well I must be, to…"

"Guys, c'mon, let's get on with it." Maddock waved his light on the engravings.

"Fine." Fabi turned back to the writing and took down some notes. It was Bones who spoke next, while pointing to the wall.

"I see this word more than once. Does it mean what I think it means?"

Fabi considered the series of characters. "*Demonio.* It does mean 'demon'."

Maddock took a close-up shot of the etched word, then checked his watch. "We should get out of here. Boat, storm..."

The four of them got the point and filed out of the holding cell into the main chamber. After a final look around to be certain they hadn't overlooked anything that could be a potential clue, they exited to the low chamber by which they had come, the only way out leading from the room. Retracing their steps, the treasure hunters made their way back through the corridor until they reached the torture chamber again.

Shining his light around the space, Maddock looked for signs of either Willis or at least of the rope that he had promised to return with. But he saw neither. He walked toward the opening and called up through it, in case Willis was hanging around just out of sight. "Willis, you there?"

But the voice that came back did not belong to Willis.

"I can hear you down there. Come here where I can see you and keep your hands visible. You're under arrest."

Chapter 12

Down in the chamber, Maddock heard Willis' voice next, protesting loudly. A little too loudly, Maddock thought. "Man, I told ya'll my friend done fell through! I'd say it's your job to help him out but I don't believe you two are real cops."

Maddock heard another voice answer Willis. "We saw you with a girl. We'd like to meet her." Laughter followed. Something about the way the man said the word "girl" told Maddock these men were up to no good. Bones moved next to Maddock and they exchanged looks.

"What do we do?" Bones whispered to avoid being heard, since so far it seemed that the unknown men were aware only of Willis' and Fabi's presence. Before Maddock could answer, a voice called down.

"You, girl! Come out where we can see you. Don't try anything funny or we'll have to shoot up that pretty body."

Fabi sidled up next to Maddock and Bones, still beyond the newcomers' line of sight down the hole. Maddock whispered, "I've got an idea." He proceeded to relay it. Then Fabi nodded and moved beneath the hole into the beam of the man's flashlight.

A rope dropped down through the hole to the chamber floor. Fabi picked it up and made a show of tentatively grasping it and attempting to climb. She called up through the hole. "I don't think I'm strong enough to climb this."

They heard Willis' voice from somewhere out of sight. "Untie me and I'll pull her up myself. Y'all look like you can't pull nothing but your own…"

"Shut up!" two different unseen male voices said in turn. A new face appeared at the top of the hole, eyes squinting as the man's eyes adjusted to the dim light. Maddock and Bones slid into the shadows behind a torture rack while Fabi remained with the rope. One of the unknown voices yelled down from above.

"Tie a loop in the rope and step into it."

Fabi hesitated. "Sorry, but it's going to take more than one of you to pull me up. I'm not a skinny gal."

Maddock watched from his place of concealment as a second set of hands appeared at the top of the hole. He put a hand on Bones' shoulder, a signal that meant *get ready*. The two men above reached down and began to lift Fabi on the rope. Maddock watched until her feet cleared the floor, and then he and Bones sprung.

Maddock reached the rope and heaved on it, while Bones leapt off a pile of fallen rock like he was making a basketball layup. The tall Indian reached up and grabbed each of the two men pulling on the rope by a wrist and yanked, hard. The two men fell twelve feet from the top of the hole to hit the ground. They lay there a moment, stunned.

Maddock and Bones used the opportunity to knock them fully unconscious, and then they tied them up with their boot laces. When they were finished they looked up to see Willis peering down through the hole, waving.

Bones waved back. "I thought your hands were tied?"

"I got loose. Who do y'all think gave those fellows a push from behind? Nice assist, though, Bones. Now go ahead and step into the loop, for real, and I'll pull you up. Ladies first."

Fabi allowed Willis to haul her up out of the torture chamber. They repeated the process with Bones and then Maddock, who asked Willis if there could be other intruders where those had come from.

"Just those two bozos."

Maddock reiterated the need to get back to their boat. While the rain had let up some, the wind was now more forceful than before. They left the fort grounds and made their way back through the jungle, Willis in particular very wary of monkeys. But they emerged from the narrow path onto the beach without incident, only to be greeted by an unexpected sight.

A simple wooden boat with a large outboard motor lay beached up on the sand, not far from their dinghy. Maddock headed for the unknown craft.

"I'm guessing this is the boat your fan club took out here, Fabi." He reached the open vessel and began searching it, rummaging through the console to see if he could find an ID. The others joined him and they overturned life jackets, a cooler, coils of rope. It didn't take long for Bones to come up with something. He held it up: a solid brick of white powder.

Willis raised his eyebrows. "Bones, you gonna share some of that? Because that's a little too much for one person."

"Well, there's Fabi..."

She shook her head and was about to say something when Maddock cut them off by taking a rope from the drug boat and tossing it to Willis. "Tie this off to the dinghy. Bones, help me push this thing out."

Bones threw the block of powder into the water and the men shoved the boat out into the water until it floated while Willis connected the tow rope. Maddock pulled the dinghy out into the water and then got in it. "C'mon, let's drag this thing out to sea, buy ourselves a little more time."

With all four in the dinghy, they motored out into the bay, towing the drug boat behind them. When they neared the *Sea Foam*, they undid the rope, casting the interlopers' boat adrift. Then they boarded the *Sea Foam* and pulled the dinghy aboard.

Maddock got behind the wheel and fired up the engine. "We need more information. Let's get back into town and see what else we can learn about this sailor held prisoner."

Chapter 13

Petit-Trou-de-Nippes

The ripe smell of fish hung over the market that dominated the waterfront in the town's modest commercial district. The four of them wandered through it, Fabi pointing out local delicacies to Bones and Willis while Maddock remained singularly fixated on their current objective: finding the elderly fisherman who was reputed to know all of the local legends and lore.

Upon arriving back at town and securing the boat, they had first visited the library. Fabi had explained to the librarian that they sought information about a sailor from long ago, and the librarian had referred them to an individual she said they would find at the fish market.

Far from an industrial scene like the seafood exchanges of Tokyo or even Havana, the market here was casual and mostly sedate. A line of crude wooden stalls were erected near the water, with a few fishermen still unloading the day's catch. They unloaded nets and ice chests from dories and pulled up to the beach, haggling with the vendors in good-natured fashion. A gaggle of locals perused the offerings, which were often placed in burlap sacks for the trip home. Besides many types of fish, there were also oysters, clams, crabs, lobster, and shrimp on display.

Maddock eyed the fishermen he passed, but most of them, while adult males, were not what he would call elderly. He and the others traversed the length of the market without seeing a likely candidate. He turned around, looking for anyone who might help him find an elderly fisherman knowledgeable about local maritime history. He was about to admit they would just have to start approaching people at random when he spotted someone lying down on the deck of a weather-beaten fishing boat. The vessel lay right off the beach, in water so shallow it was barely floating, and its sole occupant reclined on a pile of nets. An old man.

"Old man and the sea, there?" Bones gave a subtle nod of the head.

Maddock nodded. "Fabi..." He looked over toward the boat, indicating that her language skills would likely be required. He asked Bones and Willis to wait in the market so that they wouldn't appear too intimidating, four people boarding the boat at once.

"No problem," Willis said. "We'll keep an eye on you from here."

"Maybe keep an eye on some of these shrimp, too." Bones began chatting up a seafood vendor, pointing to the tasty crustaceans, while Maddock and Fabi waded out into ankle deep water until they were in a position to board the fishing boat.

"What's this guy's name again?" Maddock asked in a low voice.

"She said it was Jean-Claude Panier. I'll do the greeting, you just smile and look friendly."

"Got it."

Fabi ascended the short boarding ladder and said something in Creole. The old man, who wore only a pair of rolled-up trousers stained with fish blood, and whose hair and beard were stark white, rose to a sitting position atop his mound of netting. He answered back in the same language while pointing to the vendor stands on the beach.

"He thinks we want fish," Fabi translated for Maddock. She turned back to the fisherman and said something else, at the end of which the man waved them aboard. Maddock followed Fabi onto the deck of the old boat, which reeked of fish and saltwater and fuel. Maddock smiled and nodded to Panier, who nodded in return but did not bother to stand up.

Fabi spoke at length in Creole and then the man's eyes seemed to light with recognition. He said some words in Creole with a raspy voice that had experienced much rum over the decades, and then Fabi turned to Maddock.

"He says he has heard a story of a 'mad sailor' who claimed to know the location of a shipwreck treasure—a very valuable one with many coins—that locals have searched for extensively but never found any trace of."

The old man nodded at Maddock when Fabi paused, as if to assert that what he had said was true even though he could not understand the translation. Panier then added some more detail, which Fabi again passed on to Maddock.

"Now he says that either the sailor was lying or the shipwreck must be a long way from here, because if it was anywhere around here someone would have found it by now."

Maddock and Fabi exchanged a glance while the fisherman remained silent, watching them.

"Ask him if he knows anything else...any other details at all." Maddock made eye contact with the man as he said this, to show that he was serious, that this was an important matter to him. The mariner flexed his toes in the netting while he appeared to think about it. At length, he nodded and spoke with deliberation.

"There is one more thing," Fabi relayed. The old man spoke again and Maddock watched Fabi's eyebrows rise. Then she translated.

"He says that, according to local teachings, a priest came to exorcise the sailor of his demons. He persuaded the French to let him take the sailor with him. They went to the cathedral in Hinche, here in Haiti.

Maddock nodded . It was something to go on. He said thank you to the man in French, then turned to Fabi and told her they should get going. But before they could leave, the old fisherman raised a hand and spoke rapid fire Creole. It didn't sound like a routine *Thanks for stopping by, glad I could be of help*, kind of thing, so he looked to Fabi for an explanation.

"He cautions us to watch out, for *the evil walks the trail of the lost treasure*."

Maddock nodded. "We've heard about the demons."

The fisherman apparently recognized the last word,

because he quickly uttered one of his own while shaking his head.

Fabi almost whispered the words to Maddock. "He says they're not demons."

"Then what are they?"

The old man repeated the key word without awaiting Fabi's services.

Zombii.

Chapter 14

Hinche

The Cathedral of the Immaculate Conception was not what Maddock had envisioned. He expected a centuries-old facade, but this building, while clearly a cathedral, was a prime example of modern architecture. Two large towers bookended an elaborate framework of arches.

He searched for the words to describe it. "This place is…"

"…funky," Bones finished.

"It does have a real on-again-off again history," Fabi said.

"Kind of like us?" Bones grinned.

Fabi smirked. "Kind of like that, I suppose, but over a much longer time period. Construction began in the 1500s as a parish church, when the town boomed with the discovery of gold. But some years later, after the gold mines had been depleted, the town was abandoned before the church was completed. It sat around unfinished all the way until the 1800s, when construction took up again, but with a new design. Even then it didn't actually get finished until the early 1900s."

"So what's it used for today?" Bones asked as they walked toward the front entrance.

"Church services. Let's get inside and see if anyone can help us."

The front doors were wide open and so they entered a cavernous main room lined with long pews. No service was in progress but a couple of people sat quietly with their heads down near the back, and a priest stood off to the side. Fabi, Maddock, Bones, and Willis approached the priest, who initially spoke with Fabi in Creole but quickly shifted to English, perhaps sensing that the three men in Fabi's party didn't speak the native tongue.

"I have a room where we can talk without interrupting the worshippers." He turned and walked down the aisle until he reached a door. He opened it and led the group inside. A few chairs were scattered about, and another door led into a confessional booth.

The priest, an elderly black Haitian who explained he had been schooled in the Bahamas where he learned to speak English, asked them what he could help them with. Maddock told the story of the crazy sailor from the 1700s, and then the priest's eyes seemed to twinkle with recognition.

"Yes, I have heard that tale. The sailor's name was reputed to be Alonso Sanchez. He did eventually regain his sanity and left the island." The priest held up a long, bony finger before continuing. "Here is the funny thing, though: Even as his mind returned, Sanchez insisted the demons he had 'experienced' were real. He never recanted his testimonial that he saw some sort of... 'demons', was the word he was always recorded having used."

Maddock asked a few more questions, but the priest had nothing more substantial to offer, and so they thanked him for his help and exited the room. On the way out through the cathedral, Maddock couldn't help but notice two more doors, both set into the front wall of the church, behind the pulpit and stage, which featured a small band setup, including a drum set and organ.

Maddock said nothing, however, as the priest walked out of the room into the aisle, watching them leave. They left the building the way they had come and walked out to their vehicle. After they had gotten in, Fabi at the wheel, Maddock recapped what they had learned, which was not much more than the sailor's name.

Bones shook his head and gave a heavy sigh. "I had high hopes for that place. What's your fall back plan if this treasure hunting thing doesn't work out, Maddock? I think I might try out for the Raiders."

Willis laughed heartily. "Funniest thing I've heard all

day. I would enjoy watching you get crushed out there, though."

This triggered an argument until Maddock spoke over them to stop it.

"Don't suit up for the field just yet, Bones. I don't think we're quite done here."

"What do you mean?" Fabi looked over from the wheel.

"You said they added on the new church to the old cathedral, right?"

"Correct."

"So maybe we should find a way to have a look at the original structure. Could be that part of it is still down there, but sealed off. If we could only find a way in..."

Bones appeared skeptical. "The priest was a nice guy, he didn't mind hearing us out and talking to us for a bit, but something tells me he wouldn't be too keen on giving us the keys to the kingdom."

Maddock turned around in the front seat to look back at Bones and Willis. "What if we came back later after he's not there?"

Night fell a few hours later and the four of them returned to the cathedral after a light supper. They saw no activity outside, only a cone of light from a fixture over the door. As they approached, Maddock asked Fabi if she thought it would be open. She shrugged. "Maybe, maybe not. There are churches whose doors are always open, but it's not uncommon for some to lock up after hours. Vandalism and theft can be a problem here, especially for the nicer places, and I'd say this is one of the nicer ones."

"Time to find out," Willis said as they walked up to the front door again. He pulled on the handle but the double door wouldn't budge.

Fabi breathed a sigh. "Really sorry, guys."

Willis gave her a shocked look. "I thought you said you and Bones were a thing?"

Confused, she half-stammered out a reply. "Were, sometimes, whatever. What's the point?"

Willis stepped aside from the door and let Bones take his place. "You would think you knew the man a little better. Bones don't need no key, do you, my man?"

"Doubt it. Let me take a look." Bones went to work on the door while Maddock and Willis kept watch. Bones pulled a folding multi-tool from his pocket and applied it to the door lock. A soft click sounded, and when Bones tried the knob, it turned. He pushed the doors open, looked inside to make sure no one was there, then stepped over the threshold.

The others followed him in and Willis shut the door behind them. A few lights were on inside, making it possible to see enough to move around, but it was still very dim. Maddock urged them in a low voice that if someone should emerge from one of the rooms , they should say they found the door open and came in to pray. But as they moved toward the front of the church, no one did come out, nor could they hear anything to indicate someone else might be here. They reached the stage behind the pulpit, where Maddock had seen the two doors.

Maddock said that he and Willis would check the door on the left while Bones and Fabi took the one on the right. "First thing is to see if we'll need Bones' special skill set," Fabi said as she tried the door knob. But it opened, and she and Bones checked it out while Maddock opened the other door.

"It's just a broom closet," Fabi called out right away.

"Maybe we should hang out in here a little while, make sure we don't miss anything in here," Bones joked.

"Get a room, you two," Willis called from the one he and Maddock had just entered.

Maddock found a light switch and flipped it on, bathing the place in low light from a single overhead fixture. "Office." He took in a neatly organized wooden desk, a large, ornate cross featuring a life-sized Jesus nailed in place hanging on one wall, a group of framed pictures showing the priest they had talked to giving sermons, and others that were historical photos of the cathedral in different stages of construction.

Willis began rifling through the desk drawers while Maddock studied the walls and floor, which was a contemporary, though unremarkable, tiled affair. Bones and Fabi appeared in the doorway, taking in the small room.

"Exciting." Bones looked to Willis. "I take it the desk isn't full of gold doubloons?"

Willis held up a worn bible and a box of candles, shaking his head. "Get that throwing arm warmed up, Bones. This treasure hunt thing's looking more and more like…"

"Look here." Maddock walked to the big cross. It was so large that it rested on the floor while the top of it came just shy of the ceiling. He peered behind the cross and noticed that there was a millimeters-wide space between it and the wall.

"You thinking about repenting or something, Maddock?" Willis watched him put both hands on the cross and begin to put pressure on it.

"Too late for that..." Maddock pushed and then pulled the religious symbol, but nothing happened.

"What, you think it's hiding something behind it? Is there something there?" Fabi walked over to him.

"Just a tiny gap. But this thing is solid wood, very heavy, so I'm wondering why it doesn't hang flush against the wall. Also curious as to why such a big cross is locked away in here instead of out in the main church." Maddock pulled up on the cross, but again it didn't budge. "It's almost like they—"

As he pulled down on the life-sized crucifix, they heard a *thump* as the bottom of the wood hit the floor. The tile beneath the cross flipped up smoothly until it came into contact with the wooden post, revealing a dark open space wide enough for a person to fit through with a ladder leading down.

"What the..." Willis moved from the desk over to the exposed trap door.

"Is it just a hiding place for the priest's secret stash, or does it actually lead anywhere?" Bones also crossed the room, eager for the answer to his own question. Maddock had already produced his flashlight and had the beam aimed down into the uncovered space.

"Looks like it leads somewhere."

"Let's not get our hopes up too much," Fabi cautioned. "I'd like to think it leads down to the old cathedral, but it could just be a basement."

"A hidden basement with a secret trapdoor?" Willis held the light for Maddock so that he could climb down using both hands.

"We'll find out soon enough." Maddock descended the rungs of the old wooden ladder. "Tunnels! Come on down," he called up. Willis closed the office door and then he, Bones and Fabi joined Maddock below.

"Catacombs." Fabi surveyed the dank stone walls. They followed the unlit passage until it branched right and left.

"I see cells up ahead to the left," Maddock said. "Let's check those out."

They walked left, the sound of water dripping on the stone floor echoing weakly in the catacombs. Two cells were set into the left side of the passage, iron doors swung open. Maddock and Willis walked into one while Bones and Fabi entered the other.

"They sure were big on the leg irons in those days, weren't they?" Willis shook his head as he eyed the now familiar heavy iron fixtures embedded into the wall.

"Big on carving stuff into walls, too." Bones' voice echoed through the catacombs. "Looks like somebody was writing a novel in here. Take a look."

After a quick look, Maddock and Willis revealed nothing noteworthy inside their cell. They joined Bones and Fabi in the adjacent one. Maddock added his light to Bones' on the rear wall. Dense lines of symbols engraved into the stone blocks challenged them as to their meaning.

Bones shook his head. "It's all Greek to me."

"There's the 'demon' word again." Fabi pointed it out. "Here...here...and there."

"Wait a minute." Maddock zoomed in on a section of the engravings with his light. "I think I do recognize a word..." He knelt on the stone floor and eyeballed the painstakingly carved glyph. He spelled it out. "Z...O...M...B...I...and another 'I'..."

"*Zombii*," Fabi completed.

Bones shone his light on the word. "We should look into zombie lore around the island, see if there's a connection to this sailor. I'd say this must be where the 'crazy' guy was held, right?"

They all agreed, but Maddock still appeared doubtful. "I agree this is where the sailor was held, but I don't know about the zombie thing, Bones. I mean, really? We're supposed to be tracking down a treasure, relying on historical facts, not urban legends or whatever you want to call them."

Willis exited the cell. "Let's see what else is down here, then. Maybe we'll find more clues."

The other three filed out and they proceeded to explore the remaining catacombs. They turned out not to be all that extensive, and only a few minutes later they had come to dead ends without discovering anything else that would aid them in their search.

Maddock met up with the others, meeting in a huddle at the junction of the two main passages. "Zombies it is. Let's get out of here and we'll head back into town to see if there's a connection to our sailor."

Fabi nodded. "Good idea. I actually need to stop by my clinic to take care of some work things, but I can give you some local contacts who might be able help you with historical zombie lore."

Chapter 15

Petit-Trou-de-Nippes

Fabi sat at a computer in the office of the local health clinic. On the screen in front of her was a database, one she had designed herself, that contained patient data and which tracked visits by searchable criteria. She was in the middle of making modifications to the design when a knock came at the door to the office, even though it was open.

She saved her work and turned around to see a tall, well-dressed man standing in the doorway. His immaculately coiffed dark hair, straight white teeth, and fine features immediately set him apart. In this part of Haiti, a man dressed in a suit was an unusual sight, but knowing who he was, his atypical appearance didn't surprise her. Ricardo Avila, a wealthy doctor who funded the clinic, was somewhere in his fifties but fit for his age. Well known for his public funding campaigns, the physician was not very hands on with this particular clinic. In fact, Fabi could recall only one other time she'd ever seen him here, and that was when she had first started work.

Avila walked over to the desk and extended a hand. Fabi rose from her chair, wondering what this was about.

"Miss Baptiste, please accept my sincere condolences on the death of your beloved cousin, David. His loss is a tragedy to the entire community. Such a good, pious man."

Fabi hesitated longer than she usually would to give thanks, because in her mind she was wondering how Avila even knew she was related to David. "Thank you."

"Were you two close?"

His eyes always looked as if they were almost closed, making it hard to judge the sincerity of his expressions, but as far as Fabi could tell, he seemed genuinely interested.

"We were, yes. I have many fond memories of growing

up with David and playing as kids here in Haiti."

Avila pointed to an empty chair next to the desk, one Fabi kept there for visitors who needed to sit with her while she helped them with something on the computer. "May I?"

"Of course." Fabi pulled the chair out for him and he took a seat.

He cleared his throat before speaking, looking her directly in the eyes through his half-closed lids as he did. "Tell me Fabiola, when was the last time you saw your cousin? Alive, I mean."

She recoiled a little, taken aback by the somewhat alarming question. "Why would you ask such a thing, Dr. Avila?"

He physically backed off a bit, pulling away from her in his chair. "I apologize for being so intrusive. I do not mean to pry on a personal level. It is just that I have a bad habit, I guess you could call it, of being overly familiar with people. In fact, I guess it's fair to say I'm such a people person that I like them a little too much."

"Well, as you know, my permanent residence is in Miami, so I hadn't actually seen him in a few months, but I did talk to him by phone a few weeks before."

Avila seemed to consider this for a moment, nodded and then continued. "The reason for my visit is because I've heard glowing reports about your work here at the clinic." He indicated the computer. "The databases you've developed have been a tremendous boon to our organizational efficiency, and so I wanted to see if you might be interested in a more permanent, paid position, not only here at this clinic, but for my organization. I have other clinics throughout Haiti, some of which are larger and much better funded than this one. I have no doubt that you'd be able to make even more of a difference there."

Fabi looked back to her computer screen, at the database application she'd worked on over the months. Her life was in Miami now. She loved her native Haiti, but she'd moved on and built a life in America. And then there was Bones. He lived in North Carolina, not so terribly far from

Florida. To relocate now... She looked away from the screen and back to Avila.

"Thank you very much for the offer, Dr. Avila. Let me give it some thought."

The doctor handed Fabi a business card and smiled. "You'll be hearing from me."

Chapter 16

Petit-Trou-de-Nippes

"I think this is it." Maddock put the old Jeep in park and looked up at the house.

"*This* is it?" Bones eyed the humble abode with disbelief.

Maddock nodded while pointing a finger. "She said, 'three houses down on the right side after you turn on to the dirt road off *De La Republique*.'"

Willis nodded from the back seat. "This should be it. Let's check it out."

The three ex-Navy men got out of the vehicle and walked across the road past a few roosters over to the property. Somewhere on the street they could hear a baby crying and a dog barking, but other than that there didn't seem to be a lot of activity. A crude fence made of corrugated sheet metal surrounded the lot, but there was a section removed for a gateway. The yard wasn't landscaped, but looked nice enough with a few natural palm trees and flowering shrubs.

They mounted a shaded porch area in front and Maddock knocked at the screen door leading into the dark dwelling. He called out, "Hello? Ms. Beaublanc? Are you there?"

Fabi had given them the name of Roseline Beaublanc, a longtime local friend who was knowledgeable about Haitian folklore. While they waited for a response, Bones leaned in to examine an animal skull of some kind sitting atop a rusty 55-gallon drum. He was about to remark on it when they heard the sound of jingling bells approaching the door.

A heavyset, middle aged woman filled the doorway. She smiled, her teeth and skin almost the same shade of yellowish-brown. Her watery gaze quickly travelled from

Maddock to Willis, where it lingered for an extra second or two, to Bones, who turned away from the skull and smiled sheepishly.

"A goat," the woman said, now opening the screen door. "Was one of my favorite milkers. You must be the friends Fabi told me about. I am Roseline Beaublanc. You can call me Rose. Please do come in."

They filed through the door into the house, which, as far as Maddock could tell, did not have electricity, but once they were inside and walked to the right, he could see that the back of the shack was open to a rear porch area which let light inside. A few candles and pungent incense also burned in the living area, where a couch sat against one wall with a simple table in front of it. Rose indicated it and asked them to please have a seat. They did, Bones and Willis scuffling momentarily over who would get the middle spot, with Willis winning that battle.

Rose sat in an overstuffed recliner to the side of the couch. While she seated herself, Maddock marveled at some of the interesting knick-knacks she had on display in the home. Besides a number of paintings of saints, there were lots of natural items—feathers hanging from the wall, seashells on shelves, a turtle shell being used as a bowl on a table...Musical instruments, too—an acoustic guitar hung on the wall, an assortment of hand drums lay about. In one corner an altar of sorts occupied a table, with a sculpture of a saint and various bottles filled with liquids whose contents Maddock could only guess at. There was too much to take in before Rose began the conversation.

"My dear friend Fabi tells me you three are interested in learning about some of our Haitian religion, folklore and spirits, yes?"

Bones and Willis exchanged glances. "Spirits?" Bones blurted.

"Not the kind you drink, sweetheart."

Bones nodded and Rose went on. "You will find a number of religions and spiritual practices in Haiti. I myself am a practitioner of *Vodou*, meaning that I am what you would call a spirit servant. I give a voice to those who no longer have one."

Bones' eyes widened while Willis sat openly slackjawed.

"Wait a minute," Bones said. "You mean, voodoo is *real*?"

Rose smiled at him. "*Vodou* is as real as you or me. As real as the Earth itself. What we cannot see is still there, friends. You need only to learn how to call it."

"Can you make me a little doll of this guy?" Bones indicated Willis, then stabbed at his palm with his pointer finger. Maddock gave him a disapproving stare, but Rose seemed unfazed by the question.

"The power of *vodou* is real, but you must not take it lightly." She gave him a stern look for a moment but then transformed it into a warm smile. "I know you are good people. I can feel it."

Bones nodded. "Thanks. So what about *zombii*? Are they as real as *vodou*?"

Rose stayed quiet for a moment, her warm look transforming back into a hard stare. "*Zombii* are not, and never have been, a part of *vodou*."

It didn't escape any of them that she hadn't answered the second part of Bones' question. Maddock focused the line of inquiry by asking Rose if she could tell them anything else about *zombii*. "Perhaps the source of the legends, if the legends are more common to one part of the island than others..." Maddock trailed off suggestively, and she took the bait, raising a finger.

"I will tell you about it. *Zombii*, as well as your *vodou* dolls..." She paused to look right at Bones, who actually flinched under her gaze. "...are conjured by those we call 'bokor'. You might call them sorcerers. But never by *vodou* priests, because only someone very, very evil will intentionally create a *zombii*."

Maddock looked to Bones and Willis. Neither of them seemed to have anything to add, so he thanked the *vodou* priestess for her time. They got up to leave but she waved them back down.

"I have more to tell you, but first I would like to read your future. Will you let me do that?"

Willis shook his head. "Sorry, ma'am, but that just ain't my thing."

Rose gave him a long, level look. "You may go, then." She held her arm out, palm up, toward the porch. "Besides," she said, turning to Maddock and Bones. "It is these two whose souls are troubled."

"I'll wait outside, guys." Willis left the abode and then Maddock and Bones sat back down on the couch. Rose pulled her chair over so that she sat directly in front of them.

"Take my hands." Maddock held one and Bones the other. Then Rose took a deep breath, closed her eyes, and began to chant softly. Maddock was less than comfortable with the scenario, but the woman had helped him and so he didn't want to be a spoil sport. He looked briefly over at Bones, who seemed to go right along with it, closing his eyes and relaxing.

Maddock forced himself to do the same, but soon he felt a cool breeze and opened his eyes in time to see the candles flicker. Rose was swaying back and forth, eyes closed, trance-like. After a time, the priestess released their hands and picked up a wooden bowl. She shook it gently and Maddock swore he could *feel* her whispered chant and the rattling of the bowl washing over him.

Rose dumped the contents of the bowl onto the table, spilling chicken bones, shells, and pebbles onto the rough surface. She gazed at them through glassy eyes until Maddock and Bones exchange puzzled glances. Had she gone into some kind of psychotic trance? What if she didn't snap out of it? Just as Maddock was about to express these very concerns, her head snapped up, her eyes clear.

Rose turned first to Bones. "The man is not lost; he is trapped. Release him."

Then she faced Maddock. "Tragedy waits at the end of every path. Harden your heart but do not turn to stone." Then she lowered her head as if in prayer.

After a long silence, Maddock cleared his throat. "Thank you for that, Rose. You said there was more you had to tell us about *zombii*."

She slowly raised her head, a smile that Bones would later describe as "creepy, dude" spreading across her face.

"Yes, there is only one more thing. Before you called the *zombii* a legend. That is wrong. They are very real."

Chapter 17

Petit-Trou-de-Nippes

Fabi pulled up to the house, ready to unwind after a long day at work and eager to hear how Bones, Maddock and Willis had fared with the priestess. Perhaps she'd even talk Bones into giving her a shoulder rub, provided he agreed not to let his hands drift.

"Right. That'll happen," she muttered as she cut the engine.

She found the front door ajar and shook her head. *Three grown men and every one of them was raised in a barn.* But as soon as she stepped over the threshold she knew something was terribly wrong.

Furniture lay overturned. Framed pictures removed from the wall, their backs slashed open. Rugs pulled up, the contents of drawers emptied onto the floor, broken glass all over the place...

She froze in the entranceway. What if whomever had done this was still inside? Suddenly frightened for her safety, Fabi turned and ran back out of the house. She had almost reached her car in the driveway when another vehicle turned onto the street and headed in her direction. She crouched behind her car in case it was whomever had perpetrated the breaking, entering, and destruction of the property now returning, but as the vehicle approached she recognized it as the Jeep she'd loaned to Bones.

Breathing a sigh of relief, she stepped out from behind her car and waved both hands in a distress signal. Maddock pulled up right next to her, killed the engine, and the three men got out. Bones walked over to give her a friendly hug but could immediately see that something was wrong.

"The house—someone turned it upside down. I just got here five minutes ago and I was afraid to stay inside in case whoever did it is still in there."

The three ex-SEALS eyed one another, immediately transforming into operator mode. Maddock told Fabi to get into her car and lock the doors until they came back for her. Then they split up, Maddock going in straight to the front door while Willis went around the right side of the house toward the back, and Bones the left.

Each of them carried pistols, and they held them at the ready now.

Maddock reached the house first and slipped inside, remaining silent. He stepped past the entranceway into the living room so as to be visible from only one direction. He crouched and listened for signs of an intruder, but heard nothing. He knew Bones and Willis would have reached the back door by now and would be covering that. Maddock moved through the house cautiously, head on a swivel, until he reached the kitchen. That clear, he moved through it into an adjoining laundry room which had a back door out to the yard, open, the window smashed out.

"It's me, this room clear." Maddock let Bones and Willis know he wasn't an intruder before reaching for the door and opening it.

"Clear out here," Bones said, entering the house. Willis followed, and then Maddock closed and locked the back door, even though the window had been busted out. In a low voice, Maddock explained that he had not yet checked the bedrooms or bathrooms, and to proceed with operational caution.

The three of them spread out throughout the house, first moving to the unchecked areas, clearing them, and then double-checking everything again.

"We're all clear." Maddock nodded toward the front yard. "Go get Fabi and bring her in." Bones left while Maddock and Willis surveyed the damage. At length, Willis shook his head.

"Somebody sure was after something in here. This isn't the work of an ordinary thief, no way."

"I agree. Let's see what she has to say about it."

Maddock looked toward the front door, where Fabi and Bones were walking in, the shocked look still on Fabi's face.

"Thank you for making me feel safe." Fabi hugged Maddock and Willis in turn.

Maddock glanced around at the destruction then back to Fabi. "Unfortunately, I worry that by us being here looking for treasure, we're making you less safe. Do you get the feeling that someone knows your cousin may have sent you something before he died?"

Fabi nodded. "Let me check something. Come with me." She moved to the living room where an old rolltop desk lay overturned on the floor. She frowned as she looked at it. "I'm guessing they're gone..." She stooped down to the floor and began rummaging through the desk drawers....

Maddock's eyes widened. "Don't tell me...."

She looked up from the desk, her eyes red rimmed. "They took the papers that were in the cigar box."

Bones and Maddock made noises of distaste, but Willis looked puzzled. "Wait a minute. That box wouldn't fit in those drawers..."

"I took the papers out of the box and stored them in here. I'm sorry, I never thought anyone would go to such lengths to get them."

Maddock patted his pants pocket. "At least I have pictures of the critical pages, most of them, anyway."

Bones didn't look much happier in spite of that news. "Now we're in a race against...someone...to figure out those clues and get to the treasure."

Maddock looked to Fabi. "Any idea who that *someone* might be? Enemies of David's? Of yours?"

Fabi thought for a moment before shaking her head slowly. "Me, no. Not that I'm aware of, at any rate. David...also none that I know of, but for years he'd been living here while I was in Miami, so it's not impossible he got involved with something I didn't know about. He was my cousin, we were reasonably close, but not super-close."

Maddock nodded. "Okay, so we both have the same information to go off of. But it hasn't led us to the treasure so far. Hopefully, it will be just as hard for whoever stole the documents."

"I still think the zombies have something to do with it all," Bones said.

Maddock shrugged. "Maybe we are overlooking something there. I've got an idea. Fabi, where's the phone?"

"Hopefully whoever busted in here didn't cut the line." Willis narrowed his eyes.

Fabi led them into the kitchen where a cordless digital phone lay overturned on the counter, as though it had been knocked from its charging cradle. She picked it up, held it to her ear and pronounced there was still a dial tone. She handed it to Maddock and he dialed a number. While it was ringing, he explained to Fabi.

"Calling an old friend, Jimmy Letson. He was in the SEAL BUDS training with us, but he dropped out halfway through—they call it 'ringing out' because you literally ring a bell to formally quit. He's a good guy, though, went on to be a journalist, has done a lot of research and knows about a ton of things. I gave him a heads up earlier that I might need his help. Hopefully…"

Maddock cut himself off and held up a finger, indicating someone had picked up on the other end.

"Hey, its me. You find anything?" A brief pause. "No, of course I don't take you for granted." Another pause. "Two bottles? You got it."

Maddock turned to Fabi and made a scribbling motion, meaning he needed to take notes. She found a pad and pen on the floor that had been tossed out of a drawer and gave them to Maddock, who set the pad on the counter and began to write.

For the next few minutes, she and the others heard him say a lot of, "Uh huh...okay...yeah..." punctuated by occasional requests for clarification, such as, "And that perspective is unique to Haiti or more universal?"

When the topic of conversation had run its course, Maddock thanked him and hung up the phone.

Willis wasted no time. "What'd he say?"

Maddock took a deep breath and eyeballed his notes for a moment before speaking. "He knows a lot about zombies in general, not all specific to Haiti," he said, directing the last part of the statement to Fabi. He didn't want to offend her by requesting outside help besides her local contacts, but Maddock and Bones had relied on Letson more than once to get them out of a jam, and he had always come through for them.

"Out with it, Maddock," Bones prompted.

Maddock nodded, looked at his notes one more time, then summed up what Letson had told him. "So basically there are different takes on the classic zombie myth depending how you look at it. For example, a psychologist might see a zombie as simply a personification of a mental condition where a person feels overworked. Slaves, for example, reported feeling like dead men walking, merely going through the motions of being alive without actually living. A pharmacologist, on the other hand, would suspect a drug-induced state responsible for feeling dull and causing a general lack of vitality."

Fabi looked impressed. "Makes sense. There is of course a strong slave history in Haiti. Many of the first African slaves were brought to Hispaniola."

Maddock nodded. "But *zombii* can also be considered from other angles, such as scientific. There is biological basis for zombiism, including in the animal world, like ants that are taken over by fungi and other examples of extreme parasitism. "

"Cool," Bones interjected.

"And of course, there's the occult." Maddock looked at them to make sure he still had their attention, then consulted his notes again. "The word 'occult' basically means secret or hidden, and there are many spiritual practices that fall under the occult..."

Willis cleared his throat and looked at Fabi. "As we saw with your friend, Rose."

Fabi smiled. "Thought you might like her!"

Maddock continued. "She was helpful, and in fact I

think I see how something she said ties together with what Jimmy told me about the occult." Maddock got three blank stares, so he went on. "Rose mentioned that only evil practitioners of *vodou* will create a zombie. Jimmy told me that a person put into a voodoo trance will meander around in a lifeless daze. So it makes sense to me that, here in Haiti, there could possibly be a group of people creating zombies on purpose—but that the exact definition of *zombii* may be subject to interpretation."

Bones shook his head. "That doesn't give us a lot to go on, Maddock. We need a direction, here."

"That's only the background. You know Jimmy. His research is deep, and he gets very specific, especially with a bottle of Haiti's finest rum on the line."

No one said anything, prompting Maddock to continue. "Jimmy says he's still working on this, so I'll stay in touch, but he uncovered a few interesting things already. For instance, he found mention of our crazy Spanish sailor's name, Alonso Sanchez, in reference to a man living in Cap-Haitien around the same timeframe."

Fabi and Bones raised their eyebrows while Willis furrowed his brow. "He also discovered that there has been a rash of *zombii* reports in Cap-Haitien." Maddock let this hang until Bones asked, "*Has been*, as in recently?"

Maddock nodded. "As in the last three years."

Willis looked happy. "Here's some voodoo for you: I sense a road trip to Cap-Haitien in our near future."

Fabi held up a finger. "I've got an idea. My supervisor at the clinic where I volunteer asked me if I'd be interested in possibly going full-time at one of the larger clinics, and I know one of those happens to be in Cap-Haitien. So what I could do is take him up on his offer—I was seriously considering it anyway as a way to expand my professional reach—and then while I'm there maybe I'll be able to learn more about these *zombii* attack rumors."

Maddock looked agreeable to this. He nodded to Bones and Willis. "Jimmy also gave me a list of landmarks around Cap-Haitien that might lead to treasure clues, so we can go up there together and while Fabi is setting up shop, we can follow up on those."

Chapter 18

Cap-Hatien

Odelin picked up his cellular phone on the first ring and flipped it open. The voice on the other end was no-nonsense, instructing him to be on the lookout for Fabiola Baptiste, who had just taken a new job in Cap-Hatien.

"You ought to be able to keep tabs on her, and anyone with whom she might be working."

Odelin translated "you ought to" as "you had better". He smiled. For once he was ahead of his boss.

"I'm already on it." He ended the call and peered over his local newspaper at the front door of the health clinic. He'd been staked out here for some time, watching for Fabi, but was surprised to see the three American men emerge from the front door. He scowled, wondering what they were up to, and then he placed a call on his phone.

When his contact answered, he said, "I need you to follow someone, and I need you to make it fast. Listen carefully..."

Thc old Jeep Wrangler rolled to a halt in front of Sans Souci Palace, Maddock at the wheel with Willis having won the ro-sham-bo for the shotgun seat, Bones in the back.

"Cool place." Bones admired the expansive, multi-story stone and brick structure. The former residence was set atop an expansive grassy hill, with a dirt switchback traversing part of it.

"Jimmy told me it was built in 1813 as the home of Haiti's king at the time, Henri I. It was built by slaves, many of whom were reported to have died during construction. Once it was done, it became known for hosting elaborate parties."

Bones stared up at the historical landmark, his

expression conflicted. "Normally I would say, 'Sounds like my kind of place,' but I don't know...the whole slave labor thing puts a little bit of a damper on it for me."

Willis snorted. "Just a little bit."

"One more thing," Maddock pointed out. "These days it's abandoned."

"We'll be the only ones here?" Willis asked.

Maddock shrugged. "I don't know about that. It's more or less open ruins. But it doesn't look crowded."

They saw two other vehicles parked some distance away, but no other people. They took it all in for a few moments and then Bones' features screwed up into a puzzled expression.

"Wait a minute...Isn't the timeline all wrong for our crazy sailor if this place wasn't built until 1813?"

Maddock nodded. "Jimmy told me that before the palace was built, this was the site of a plantation run by a serious bad guy, and the sailor worked there. So I figured this might be worth checking out." He nodded up the hill to the old palace.

"Bad guy how?" Willis wanted to know.

Maddock shrugged. "He didn't elaborate. I figured he was a slave-driver plantation owner type, typical for the 1700s."

Bones jumped out of the Jeep. "Let's get to it."

Chapter 19

Sans Souci Palace

The ruins of the Sans Souci Palace loomed gray and foreboding atop a high hill. Despite the fact that it was, literally, a shell of its former self, its majesty was evident in the impressive architecture and solid construction. Above a series of walled terraces, high windows and arched doorways looked out from the once ornate structure. The brick construction was visible beneath the crumbling veneer.

"They don't make them like that anymore," Bones mused.

"Yeah, but why'd they have to build it so high up?" Willis mopped his brow as he trudged up the switchback.

"Better sight lines. Makes it more defensible." Maddock eyed the towering edifice. Sunlight shone through narrow windows cut in the stone walls.

"Defensible against who, exactly?" Bones asked.

"The British. The Spanish. Maybe pirates?" Maddock resumed hiking up the trail again. They reached the front wall of the palace and had to skirt it for some distance before they found a break in its length and continued on their way up.

Once inside the palace walls, Willis whistled out of appreciation for just how expansive the property was. "Gonna take some time to check all this out. We better get moving."

Maddock agreed, but added, "I think it's doubtful there could still be anything meaningful as a clue in plain sight."

"Maybe more coded messages?" Bones thought aloud.

"Maybe. But I think we should concentrate our search by looking for something that leads down, underground. If there is anything below the palace, that's what we want to see."

"Let's spread out, then, and if we find anything that leads down we'll meet up," Bones suggested.

The three were in agreement and set off in different directions around the palace. Bones headed inside at the closest entry point to where they stood, while Willis went right around the perimeter, and Maddock went left.

Once on the opposite side of the palace from where they started, Maddock stepped inside through an open arch. Inside was empty and barren looking, leaves and debris scattered about, even a few beer bottles, cigarette butts and food wrappers. Clearly the place was visited now and again. He moved through the floor plan, which was mostly open, rooms delineated only by great open archways. He found a stairway leading up and ascended, deciding to take a quick look even though he sought a passage beneath the palace. Upstairs it looked no different than the ground floor, though, and after a rapid walkthrough, Maddock descended the stairs back to the main level.

He listened for a minute to make sure he wasn't missing anything from Bones or Willis, or anything else, but all was quiet so he continued with his reconnoitering of the first level. He passed through a series of new rooms, but they too were devoid of functional features. He moved into a smaller room at the corner of the palace. This room featured an intact staircase leading up to the second level. Maddock was considering walking up there to check out this end of the second level, when his gaze followed the stairway back down to where it met the floor, and lingered there.

On first glance he had assumed that the floor where the staircase joined it was broken up, the stone smashed by...by what, he had no idea, but there were many parts of this old palace that were crumbling. But now, on closer inspection, Maddock could see that the section of floor was comprised of a jumble of stones and rock slabs, of the same type as that of which the palace was made. Many of them were precariously stacked up against one another, and Maddock became curious as to whether they might conceal anything beneath them.

He kicked over a couple of the jagged slabs with his shoe, overturning them to reveal more rocks underneath them. He continued his excavation, kicking aside large pieces in order to reveal what lay beneath. After a few minutes he had moved aside enough rock to see that there were two smooth , intact slabs of stone, one above the other. He worked aside more rock, and then the realization hit him: he was looking at part of the stairway that led *down*, beneath the first floor.

Excited, he called out for Bones and Willis without using their names, an operational habit ingrained in him from his days as a SEAL. They signaled they had heard and were on their way, and Maddock resumed his excavation of the stairway. He proceeded carefully, assuming correctly that much of the aged staircase had crumbled and fallen away, leaving gaps and unstable spans. By the time he had uncovered enough rubble to see an open hole gaping into a black void wide enough for him to squeeze through, Bones and Willis came jogging into the room.

Maddock explained the condition of the hidden staircase. He urged them to take caution so as not to fall through, and then they proceeded to help him remove more of the rubble. The work proceeded in rapid fashion with the three former SEAL teammates working together, and in short order they had opened up enough of the stairway to get a clear look at what they were dealing with.

An opening easily large enough to accommodate a single man now yawned at their feet. Maddock aimed his flashlight down into the gap they had created.

"I see a hard floor down there, about ten feet down. But the steps are shot, so it'll have to be a hang-and-drop to get down."

"What about getting back up?" Bones asked.

"Since when are you so sensible, man?" Willis asked. "But here..." He rummaged into his pack and pulled out a rope. "Wouldn't you know it, I saved the one from the other fort for good luck."

Willis wrapped the rope around a heavy stone block and

let the other end drop down into the uncovered space.

"Hold this." Maddock handed Willis his flashlight and Willis aimed it down into the opening as Maddock dropped into the hole.

"Drop the light down." Willis lowered it as far as he could and let it drop into Maddock's outstretched hand. He and Bones watched as he shone the beam around.

"Worth making the trip?" Bones asked.

"Affirmative. Come on down."

First Bones, then Willis joined Maddock, who still stood in the center of what they could now see was a small, roughly cube-shaped room.

"What is this place?" Willis asked.

Maddock started walking around. "Maybe a cellar?"

"Whatever it is, it looks like it doesn't have any exits except for the stairs."

"Let's make sure." Bones had been in similar situations with Maddock where they had ended up finding hidden passages. But after an extremely thorough search even he was ready to admit that this room was probably nothing more than a cellar.

The white van rolled at low speed, skirting the low-lying palace grounds. Two Haitian men occupied the van, one staring through binoculars up at the palace itself.

"They're inside the palace building now," the one with binoculars said. The driver turned right, onto the dirt switchback that led up the hill. A cacophony of groaning and thumping could be heard emanating from the rear cargo hold. The individual in the passenger seat banged his binoculars on the divider walling off the cargo space. "Quiet down back there."

The van crested the top of the hill and rolled to a stop next to the palace itself. The passenger again scanned the surroundings, including into the building through open archways, using the optics.

"These clowns have got nothing. They're wandering around in there."

"So we don't need them." The driver rolled the van even closer to the palace wall.

The passenger shook his head. "No way. Let's see how they fare against our friends."

The driver nodded and quietly opened his door. "I'll open the back doors and let them out. Should be fun!"

Chapter 20

Cap-Hatien

Fabi smiled as she eyeballed the computer program open on the monitor before her. It was the same one she had designed, and the familiar software made her feel more at home in her new work environment. Not that she felt uncomfortable or out of place so far—she had found the employees to be warm and welcoming, and it seemed like she would fit right in here. Not only that, but she shared an office with a co-worker with whom she got along well.

Cassandra Damas was a city girl, born and raised in Port Au Prince, relocating to the Cap-Hatien area as an adult. Fabi judged her to be in her mid-thirties. The mahogany-skinned young woman sported a medium afro and favored big hoop earrings and statement necklaces. She had worked for this clinic of Dr. Avila's for several years, and throughout the day so far had filled Fabi in on everything from office gossip to work procedures to where were the best places to go for lunch. Now, comfortable that they were on friendly terms, and as they both sat at computers fine-tuning the new database system, they were comparing notes when Dr. Avila appeared at the open doorway.

"Good afternoon, ladies! Fabi, I trust you are finding your way around okay on your first day?"

Fabi wheeled around on her chair and smiled at her boss. "You bet, Dr. Avila. Cassandra here's been a tremendous help."

Avila beamed. "Excellent. Well, I don't want to keep you two from your good work. Just wanted to check in and welcome you personally to our Cap-Hatien clinic, Fabi. If you need anything, don't hesitate to reach out to me. Carry on!"

Avila left and she and Cassandra resumed discussing the

work issue they had been focusing on before he showed up. Once they had worked through it, Fabi took advantage of a lull in the work to ask Cassandra about Avila. "Does he stop by a lot, or only on someone's first day?"

Cassandra raised her eyebrows. "He's here a lot. Especially lately, he's really been burning the midnight oil. I go home normal hours, you know, four or five, and he's always still here when I leave. And when I get here in the morning, eight or so, he's already been up and running for some time."

"Not always easy being the boss, right?"

Cassandra shrugged. "I guess not. Not like I would know," she finished with a laugh.

On a whim, Fabi decided to broach a different topic with Cassandra. She looked over at the woman. "Hey, can I ask you something that might seem a little strange?"

Cassandra took on an amused look and said, "No honey, I don't go that way, if that's it."

"Seriously, that's not it. It's about..." She lowered her voice and looked behind them to make sure no one was within earshot. "*Zombii.* I've heard there have been attacks recently in Cap-Hatien. Is that true?"

Cassandra shifted in her seat and pursed her lips. She stabbed at a couple of computer keys and then swiveled to look Fabi in the eyes. "Yes. But no one is taking it *seriously.*" She emphasized the last word with a Creole sing-song lilt.

"There is no actual evidence?"

"Well, no hard evidence yet, as far as I know, but I do know that the *zombii* reports coincide with the disappearances of people I have personally seen—patients here at this clinic. And then there's…"

Cassandra cut off the conversation at the sound of approaching footsteps. Two people passed by without lingering, but Cassandra didn't take up the topic again, returning instead to her work, where she concentrated on the screen. Fabi couldn't help but wonder what was going on that made her coworker so uncomfortable. She was highly rational in all other respects, but the subject of *zombii* at Cap-Hatien seemed to have unnerved her completely.

Fabi turned back to her own computer and forced herself to concentrate on her work.

Chapter 21

Sans Souci Palace

Maddock had given up on tracing a tiny crack in the wall when he noticed Bones had frozen, standing stock still. He knew the man possessed an excellent sixth sense of sorts, and during their days in the SEALs, he was often the first to detect an enemy presence.

"What is it, Bones?"

No sooner had he completed the question than they heard the rumble of a vehicle approaching.

Willis headed for the rope. "We're fish in a barrel if we stay here." He made his way up the rope and then helped Bones and Maddock climb out.

"Now what?" Bones pointed to a large group of people heading their way. The vehicle had departed.

Maddock eyeballed the throng. He couldn't put his finger on it, but something about the way they moved just wasn't right. They stared straight ahead, their movements not quite robotic, but lacking the natural ease with which a person might normally stroll or even walk. The assemblage of persons reached their location at the edge of the fort. Maddock called out to them a few times in English as well as limited French, but none of the people had a vocal response other than incoherent wheezing and indistinct moans.

Suddenly one of the individuals rushed forward with surprising speed toward Bones, who sidestepped him and clocked his assailant square on the chin. It was a blow that would have knocked out any rowdy drunkard at Crazy Charlie's Saloon, but this man seemed to be barely fazed.

"Now we run!" Maddock pointed off to their right and took off at a sprint. Bones and Willis were right on his heels. They flew over uneven rock formations and clumps of dirt until they reached the palace's perimeter wall. Maddock led them to a break in the structure and paused there to gauge the progress of their pursuers—still coming, and fast.

"Let's go, this should act as a bottleneck for them." Maddock slipped through the break in the wall, again followed by Bones and Wills.

Their pursuit didn't delay much, rapidly pouring through the gap. Others appeared on either side, preventing Maddock and the others from doubling back to their vehicle. The trio ran directly uphill, often skipping the switchback trail in favor of climbing straight up.

"Up there!" Maddock shouted. Lungs burning, muscles screaming, he led the way up to a massive building—much larger and more intact than Sans Souci palace. He knew from his research that it was called the Citadelle Laferrière, another popular tourist destination. Cut off from any other escape route, the three had been forced to retreat uphill. Several times they'd tried to evade their pursuers and work their way back downhill to their waiting vehicle, but to no avail. They were hemmed in, choked off by natural landforms and nearly encircled by the line of pursuit. Maddock estimated they'd covered nearly five kilometers. Thankfully all were in excellent shape, because their pursuers had dogged their trail, not flagging for an instant. Maddock and the others had managed to widen the distance between themselves and the pursuit, but it was only a matter of time before they ran out of steam.

Bones stared up at an imposing structure. "If Sans Souci Palace was on a hill, this place is on a mountain."

Willis surveyed their surroundings in all directions. He lingered on the road behind them. "They're still coming."

"Unbelievable," Bones said. "And they've spread out, too. One of us might get past them, but not all three."

"I nominate Maddock as sacrificial lamb," Willis said.

"Yeah, right." Maddock eyed the citadel. "That gang or whatever they are will be on us soon. We don't want them to catch up to us on open road. We'll have to make our stand here."

Bones pumped his fist. "Remember the Alamo! Or somewhere the good guys actually won."

The trio moved off the road to a path that wended its way up the final stretch to the Citadelle. The way became even tougher going on the upper part of the mountain, and by the time they were near the crest, they could hear the upward progress of the horde as they crunched over brambles and knocked down rocks. The three men forged on and after a while Bones' whoop signaled that they had reached the plateau on the summit where the citadel was situated.

Before them, the high walls loomed more than one hundred feet tall. It would have afforded defenders a remarkable view of the surrounding area.

"Too bad we don't have a few sniper rifles handy," Bones said.

They moved onto a concrete strip probably once used for staging artillery. Signage nearby indicated that the old stronghold was built in 1805 as a means of defense against French invasions. The building, up close, was much more elaborately designed and more intact than the fort at Sans Souci.

"Check it out." Bones pointed to rows upon rows of round, metal balls a few feet in front of them. "Cannonballs."

"Hey Bones," Maddock said, looking down the slope, "maybe you could come back as a tourist some other time, okay? Because we don't have long before our friends down there get to us."

"He's right." Willis also looked down the mountain, his brow furrowed with concern.

Maddock looked back to the cannonballs and then down the mountain again, where the mob of non-lingual men was that much closer. "I have an idea. From watching these things, I've noticed that they can run fast, but they don't have good lateral movement. They can't turn well. It's almost like these are the..."

Willis turned to look at him. "The what?"

Maddock shrugged. "The *zombii* Rose told us about. Look at the way they move—it's like certain parts of their senses are just...*off*."

He turned and eyed the stack of old ammunition Bones had pointed out.

Bones smiled. "Hell yes. Zombie bowling."

The cannonballs, though old and rusted, came free with a little persuasion. They were heavy enough that it was only practical for each man to carry two at a time, but they made quick trips and in short order had a good sized pile perched on the concrete strip on the edge of the summit. Below them, the horde was scrambling ever closer; they could hear the ragged rasp of their breathing from those on the front line.

"Bombs away." Maddock hefted the first cannonball and gave it an underhanded toss over the mountaintop. It bounced once and then rolled smoothly until it slammed into one of the *zombii*, cutting it down at the knees. It fell face-first on the ground and attempted to crawl forward, fingers digging into the soft turf.

"Score!" Bones then lobbed the second shot, and then Willis got into the action. Soon the three men settled into a rhythm, lobbing a ball down the hill and then bending down to scoop up another without watching to see the result of the last shot. Many balls missed their mark, but enough hit so that the main thrust of the attacking pursuers was diminished.

When the defending trio had gone through all of their stockpiled ammunition, they returned once more to the main pile to grab one more cannonball each before the still climbing *zombii* would reach the summit. Returning to the edge, each took down one more marauder with a well-rolled projectile, leaving four more to scramble over the top up onto the concrete strip.

It was now clear that in order to eliminate these final four, the three treasure hunters faced a hand-to-hand fight. Bones backpedaled away from a zombie who lunged at him.

He assumed a fighting stance, legs wide, shifting nimbly from foot to foot, a knife in his right hand while his left was extended to block.

"Davy Crockett wins this time!" he said, sidestepping the zombie's crude hammer blow and then shoving him off the cliff with a swift kick.

"Still with the Alamo?" Willis grunted as he slammed an elbow into the cheekbone of another assailant, knocking him to the ground.

"That's why we're awesome!" Bones' enthusiasm was infectious, and before long all four of the attackers had either been tumbled down the mountain with the others, or else lay at their feet, incapacitated.

Maddock reached down and rifled through the pants pockets of one of them, but found no identification or objects of any kind. He stood and looked around. "We better get out of here before someone sees what happened and we get detained for questioning."

Bones and Willis agreed, and the three of them set off for a different way back down the mountain.

"Now what," Willis asked once they had started down an empty path.

Maddock's eyes focused unwaveringly on the path ahead as he answered. "Something happened to those *zombii* people to make them that way. We're going to find out once and for all what it was. More important, I want to know why they were sent after us."

Chapter 22

Cap-Hatien

Fabi squinted hard at a line on a spreadsheet open on the computer. Beside her, Cassandra was packing up, jingling her keys, shutting down her workstation. The work day was near an end, but since it was her first on the new job, Fabi was eager to make a good first impression. She had identified an anomaly in one of her new clinic's financial statements and decided to stay a little late to get on top of it while the details were fresh in her mind.

"Girl, you been working all day. Let me show you my favorite local watering hole. Cold drinks, cheap, hot food, cute guys..." Cassandra smiled.

Fabi looked over at her new co-worker and smiled warmly. "Thanks. I really would like to do that, but I've come across something I think I can fix in one of the sheets. You know how it is, it's hard to get back in gear once you leave right in the middle of it. How about tomorrow, okay?"

"They don't pay us overtime, you know."

Fabi shrugged. "I know. I guess I'm just a workaholic."

Cassandra wrinkled her nose and stared at Fabi's screen for a few moments, then shrugged. "Okay, Fabi. I hope you get it sorted out, but don't kill yourself. No one expects you to get this whole place running like a top your first day here. I'll see you tomorrow."

Cassandra left and Fabi got back to work at the computer. She didn't want to say anything about it to Cassandra, lest she was wrong or—even worse—Cassandra had somehow been a part of it—but it looked as though a substantial portion of the clinic's budget had been rerouted for the past few months into an obscure special project. She was digging deep into the databases now for more information on this project, but at every turn she hit an encrypted file, a hardware firewall or some other security measure. Finally she got a break when she cross-referenced something she read in a cached email to a data backup log file, which gave her a file name. She searched for that file and found it buried deep in an obscure directory.

Opening the file, it became apparent that the project the clinic's funds were being funneled to was one called HAITI.

Fabi leaned back in her chair and considered the name. Sounded logical enough, pretty straightforward. Probably it was some charity initiative designed to help low income people. She still wasn't sure exactly what was going on, but with the project name she was sure she could find out more, both here on the computer network and tomorrow with a little "social engineering."

Chapter 23

Tortuga Island, northwest Haiti

Maddock and Bones pulled the dinghy up onto the rocky pebble beach and tilted up the outboard motor. The *Sea Foam* lay at anchor a few yards away in deeper water. Willis remained aboard, though reluctantly. This wasn't a place to leave their boat unattended.

After getting back in touch with Jimmy, Maddock had learned from him that this location—home of yet another defense installation, Fort de Rocher, was the site of the earliest recorded zombie activity in the region. Set on a remote island off the main coast, and long associated with pirates and treasure, Maddock decided it was worth investigating in person.

Bones gave a low whistle in appreciation of the fort that dominated the island's central plateau. "Now *that* is what I call a fort."

Maddock finished dealing with the dinghy and also eyed the historic building. An imposing stone facade was situated atop a towering rock spire.

"What's the deal on this place?" Bones asked.

Maddock recalled what Jimmy Letson had told him. "This is a really old one, erected during the 1600s by buccaneers to defend against the encroaching Spanish. Two dozen cannon overlooked the natural harbor, there." He turned and pointed to where the *Sea Foam* rocked gently at anchor.

"So how do we get up there?"

Maddock squinted into the sun as he tried to pick out a route up the near vertical rise leading to the fort's plateau. "Should be a road on the other side. Let's check it out." He walked off the beach into a lightly wooded area. Passing through this was easy going, and soon they emerged onto a plain of knee-high grass that directly abutted the stone spire. Seeing no breaks in the smooth stone face, the duo made their way around the spire though the grass. As they turned the first corner and headed left along the wall, Bones suddenly cried out and began flailing his arms.

"What is it?" Maddock jumped to out to the side so as to get a better look at what was ailing Bones. "What the..."

A brown, furry blob about the size of a bean bag had dropped onto Bones' head from somewhere higher up on the wall.

"Get it off me!"

Maddock rushed to his friend's aid, but before he could reach him the big Indian rolled out from under the thing and kicked it away from him. It landed on the grass a few feet away, moving.

"Spider!" Bones yelled, watching the oversized arachnid churn its legs in the air while it lay overturned on its back. He assumed a defensive posture, still ready to fight, but he relaxed when it became clear the huge arachnid was now in its own struggle to regain its feet.

"Come on, Bones, you never shy away from a gunfight but you're scared of this brainless creepy crawly. We've got work to do." Maddock waved an arm and continued moving at a near trot along the wall.

"That's the biggest freaking tarantula I've ever seen! Weird." With that he joined Maddock on the path around the wall. "Besides, it just surprised me. I'm not…" He cut off when they heard something shuffling their way from around the next corner. Maddock stopped moving and held out a hand. They paused and listened. The shuffling noise continued, like feet sliding across bare earth, moving leaf litter and cracking twigs.

Bones drew out his knife again, and the two men advanced.

Chapter 24

An old man hobbled around the corner. Maddock, after checking his hands to see that they were free of weapons, signaled Bones to stand down. Bones exhaled heavily and sheathed his knife.

The man, a local Haitian by the look of him, merely nodded and set about continuing on his way, giving the two Americans a wide berth. Maddock watched him walk for a few seconds but then decided he might know something about this place that could help them.

"Excuse me, sir?" He didn't know if the man spoke English, but it was worth a try.

The elderly person shuffled to a stop and slowly turned around, shaking his head. "Leave me be. I got nothing you want."

Maddock held up his hands in a placating gesture. "Relax, please. We're not going to hurt you. We just wanted to ask you a few questions about this place..." He swept an arm up at Fort de Rocher, then decided he better follow up quick with something specific to engage the man.

"We're looking into some of the legends that have been told about this island, the fort."

The man's look softened somewhat. "There are many legends."

Bones, who had been looking more and more impatient, blurted out, "What about *zombii*?"

The old man moved to a lichen-covered rock and sat down. "I tell you what. There have always been instances of *zombii*, and not only humans. Animal *zombii*, too. But at some point in the last ten years they all disappeared. The human ones, anyway."

Bones sat on the ground cross-legged in front of the man so as to be eye-to-eye. "Why did they disappear?"

The longtime local shrugged. "Folks disappear all the

time. Tortuga is and has always been a hub for illegal migration, so it's expected that people will come and go, and sometimes disappear."

To Maddock, the answer seemed too simple. "Could anything else have affected it? Any other changes?"

Again, the local shook his head. "No. The only thing that was different at all was that people came in and started exporting lots of a particular local plant, a kind of fern—very primitive—that releases spores that appear to have some medicinal effect."

Bones smirked, and the old man went on. "Not long after that began, airplanes started crop-dusting regularly. Weekly at first, then monthly, until now it's twice a year. Some people take ill after the crop dusters pass by, and the government has been petitioned for answers, but they always deny they are behind it. They say they have launched an investigation, but nothing ever comes of it."

Maddock nodded, then shifted tack. "What about a legend of a lost shipwreck treasure, or a lost Spanish sailor?"

The old local cackled with gusto. "This island of Tortuga was a hotbed for piracy." He threw his hands up in the air. "One legend is much like another and ships wreck all the time."

Maddock tried a few more questions but it was clear the old man had already offered what he knew, and so they thanked him and asked him if he needed any assistance.

"I'll be fine," the oldster said as he pushed himself onto his feet from the rock. "But you boys...." His eyes took on a faraway look, as though seeing something related to their future. "You boys be careful."

Chapter 25

Cap-Hatien

Fabi heard the clinic manager—not Dr. Avila but another physician in charge of day-to-day operations— close his office door. She heard his key turn in the lock and then listened as his footsteps approached her office. The closest building exit to him was in the other direction, so Fabi guessed he was going out of his way to stop by her office, since her light was on and the door open. Anticipating his arrival within seconds, Fabi cleared her screen of the document she had been looking at and replaced it with a routine accounting form.

Sure enough, the manager—Fabi had already forgotten his name—turned into her office, jacket slung over his briefcase, keys in one hand. "Hey, Fabi—you doing all right?"

She beamed at him as if she had never had so much fun. "Oh yeah! Getting the new database up and running."

The supervisor's eyes flicked momentarily to her screen and then back to her eyes. "Glad to see you hit the ground running. But it's your first day so don't burn yourself out, okay? We like to keep our employees long-term around here."

He left and Fabi waited a few minutes before resuming her research activities—waited until she heard the outside door close, faintly heard the sound of the manager's car engine starting up. Then she got up from her desk and walked out into the hallway, looking both ways while listening carefully. She was pretty sure she was the last one in the clinic, but to be safe she did a walkthrough of the building. She didn't need anyone catching her at what she was about to try. After completing a circuit of the facility and finding it deserted, Fabi made her way to the manager's office.

His door was closed so she reached out and turned the knob, only to find it locked. Fabi found that to be a little suspicious. None of the other office doors were kept locked after hours. The building itself was reasonably secure; it had to be, since this was a health clinic where drugs were kept. But an office? The computers did contain information that could be considered sensitive—patient records, financial information—but that data was encrypted and password protected.

Maybe the manager was reluctant to leave his office open knowing that a brand new employee would be here after he left? He didn't know her, after all. But still, he was aware she had volunteered under Dr. Avila's umbrella of clinics on Haiti for some time now, and therefore should be considered trustworthy.

Fabi examined the lock more carefully. Not a serious affair like a deadbolt, but merely one of those stock doorknob locks meant more for convenience than anything else. She removed one of the bobby pins from her hair and used it to pick the lock. As a child growing up in Haiti, she'd had plenty of friends in school to show her these sort of tricks.

She stepped into the office and softly closed the door behind her. Leaving the room lights off and using a small keychain flashlight, Fabi took a quick look around the office. As expected, nothing at first glance seemed fishy. The manager had visitors to his office every day, in any case, so she wouldn't anticipate anything not above board to be in plain view.

She walked behind the desk and eyed the computer. Powered completely off. She was no technology or hacking expert, and so no way was she going to try and get into that; she knew it would be protected, and even if she could get in, she wouldn't know how to cover her tracks.

She surveyed the room again from this new vantage point. When her weak beam highlighted a rusty metal file cabinet, she moved to it. The piece of old furniture was about head high, with six deep drawers. She tried a couple of them, but they were locked. Eyeing the locking mechanism, Fabi swept a hand on top of the cabinet, but aside from a thick layer of dust, she came away empty. Then she eyed the desk again and moved back to it. Figuring these drawers would be locked, too, she tried the shallow one in the center beneath the computer keyboard. To her surprise, it slid open with a creak.

The contents were routine office supplies, but she lifted a plastic divider tray that held rubber bands and staples and smiled when she saw a small gold-colored key beneath it. She took it over to the file cabinet and tried it in the lock. It fit, and when she turned the key she felt the click of the lock disengaging.

She opened the top drawer and rapidly scanned the files it contained, held in hanging folders. These were patient records, and Fabi nodded her silent approval that they were kept in a secure fashion before moving on to the other drawers. Two more also contained patient records, while another two seemed to be devoted exclusively to routine clinic financials. Flipping through the folders in the bottom drawer, however, Fabi's features took on a puzzled expression. What were these?

After a few minutes of examination, she determined that they were one-off projects of some kind. Each had its own budget and records. She was about to close the drawer when the title card of one of the folders, each of which appeared to be named for a different project, caught her eyes.

Project HAITI.

The same one she had come across earlier in the computer file. She plucked the folder from the cabinet and moved to the desk chair where she could examine its contents more thoroughly. She had just dug in when she heard footsteps coming down the clinic hall outside.

Quickly, Fabi doused her light and snapped the folder shut. The footsteps grew louder. She pulled the chair out and got beneath the desk.

Then the sound of the walking stopped, and the door to the office opened.

Chapter 26

Tortuga Island

Safely back aboard the *Sea Foam*, still at anchor in the natural harbor, Maddock, Bones and Willis sat on deck, each with a cold bottle of the boat's stash of Dos Equis in their hands. After a few laughs over Bones' encounter with the gigantic tarantula, as well as a recapping of their conversation with the old local, talk turned to next steps. They were still no closer to finding the treasure, and it worried Maddock that he could see the frustration settling in deeper in both Willis and Bones. Especially Bones.

Yet the fact was that Maddock didn't think Tortuga was a likely spot to find the sailing ship's riches. "According to the journal, the crazy sailor drifted along, floating with the current for about eighteen hours." Maddock put a finger on a marine chart spread out on a folding table, held in place against the breeze with seashells on the corners. "Considering the prevailing wind and current patterns in the region at that time of year, he'd have been carried west-northwest, which would make it virtually impossible to end up on Tortuga instead of being carried ashore somewhere on the Haitian coast."

Bones and Willis agreed with this after a brief discussion of the finer details pertaining to the local currents. When they had finished this digression, Maddock looked up from the chart.

"Besides the probabilities we have based on current and wind patterns, we know the sailor was most likely captured on the south side of Haiti, closer to the fort where he was originally imprisoned."

Bones drained the last of his beer and tossed the empty in a bucket. "Maybe Jimmy can check that out."

Maddock nodded, his sea gray eyes alight with a twinkle.

"He's already on it."

Cap-Hatien

Fabi ducked down as a wedge of light penetrated the manager's office as the door opened. A woman's heels clacked on the floor. She drew herself into a tight ball in an effort to be as small as possible. Her mind reeled with what she was going to say if discovered. *Just looking for a file...and I got scared when I heard someone coming?* She sure hoped it didn't come to that. But then a darker thought overcame her.

This wasn't the best part of town. What if she was about to be found by some common criminal here to rob the place or worse? Her mind was running through all sorts of terrible scenarios when she heard her name being called, by a female voice.

"...Fabi? Fabi, come out! It's me, Cassandra. I know it's you; I saw you go in there and not come out again."

Beneath the desk, Fabi hung her head and breathed a huge sigh of relief. If anyone had to find her, Cassandra was the best possible person. It was still embarrassing, but infinitely better than if her manager, or God forbid—Dr. Avila—had caught her. She had no idea what she'd do then. As it was, it was going to be awkward.

"Coming." She crawled out, stood, and gave Cassandra a sheepish look.

Cassandra left the door open but didn't turn on the lights. "Fabi, what are you doing in here? You trying to get fired? Or more than fired...one time we had a part-time worker caught stealing office supplies—I'm talking really minor stuff— and Avila had him arrested. Never saw him again, even around town."

Fabi blushed. "I wasn't trying to steal anything. I was only looking for paperwork that could help me to do my job better."

Cassandra put her hands on her hips. "Oh really? Poking around our manager's office in the dark? You think I was born yesterday, honey? I like you, but don't take me for an idiot."

Fabi eyed her new friend. At least, she was really hoping she was a friend right about now and not overly loyal to Dr. Avila.

"All right, take it easy. I'll tell you everything."

Chapter 27

Off the coast of Alto Velo Island

"Don't Haiti me because I'm beautiful." Bones said to Maddock, who consulted the chart plotter on the console of the *Sea Foam* and then rolled his eyes.

"Bones, you don't know where the heck you are. We're not in Haiti anymore. We crossed into Dominican Republic waters ten miles ago."

That the island of Hispaniola was now separated into two countries did not escape Maddock, for when the crazy sailor was here, it was but an island called Hispaniola constituting no country at all. Looming before them, a rocky isle jutted from the sea, taller than it was wide, a monolithic rock. Maddock couldn't think of it any other way. It was simply a massive rock in the middle of the ocean, off the southwest coast of Dominican Republic. The island was green up top, but all gray rock on the bottom third.

"You're sure this is the place?" Willis sounded a little worried. They'd endured a not unpleasant but nevertheless long voyage on the *Sea Foam* to get here.

Maddock shrugged. "Not sure, but it's as good a candidate as any. Remember that weird plant the man on Tortuga told us about?"

Willis and Bones nodded.

"Jimmy identified an island near the forts at St Louis de Sud that had high *zombii* activity and a high concentration of that plant."

"The one with the spores?" Bones eyed the nearing coastline with increasing interest.

"That's the one. Also, I've come across accounts that herbicides have been dropped there as well."

"Herbicides?" Willis also seemed drawn to the island, his inclusion in the conversation a mere afterthought.

Maddock exhaled in frustration.

"Yes, Willis, herbicides. As in, they kill plants, especially the one our old friend told us about—the one with the spores?"

Willis nodded, "Okay, I hear you. But the currents...are they right? That sailor's account of the weather...."

Bones picked up the ball, sensing Maddock was losing patience. "He predicted a drift that would place the shipwreck near this island—*Alto Velo*."

Maddock pulled out some crumpled notes and read from them. "Listen: Our sailor said he drifted past an island, one so small it was barely visible, but that it had lots of birds. He drifted for twenty-one days before hitting the zombie island."

Bones looked doubtful. "But how do we know where that is? Which island? Hispaniola has thousands. How do we know this is it?"

Maddock was undeterred as he looked out at the island. "*Alto Velo* fits the bill. For one thing, it was endowed with large guano deposits—yeah, bird crap—which was valuable as fertilizer and as a source of saltpeter for gunpowder."

"Holy crap," Bones added, "I'm suddenly feeling depressed."

Willis chuckled before answering. "What for, you finally look in a mirror?"

Bones shot Willis a look that conceded, *nice one*, but quickly moved on. "No, because now comes the boring part—running a grid pattern actually looking for this thing."

Chapter 28

Cap-Hatien

When Fabi finished talking, she was out of breath. She ended by telling Cassandra about how she watched their manager leave and deciding to see what he kept under lock and key all the time in his office, that maybe it had something to do with the disappearances. Cassandra eyed the folder Fabi had pulled from the file cabinet.

"And what's that?"

Fabi opened the folder on the desk. "It's some kind of special project called HAITI. I hadn't yet gotten a chance to look at it when I had to take cover."

Her new friend smiled. "Sorry about that, but I was a little worried about you. Let's take a look..."

Together they read through the file's contents, splitting the pages amongst them. After a few minutes Fabi stabbed a finger onto one of the papers. "Right here. You see that number?"

Cassandra squinted as she eyeballed the digits. "Yeah? What of it?"

"Earlier today I processed some payments, so I recognize it. It's the same account Dr. Avila once used to purchase some computer equipment for the main clinic. He's using it to bankroll this HAITI project, whatever it is."

"Must be some high limit he has on that card, too, judging by these expenditures." Cassandra raised her eyebrows as she traced a finger along the recorded charges. Fabi looked up from the records.

"Okay, so Dr. Avila is funding this HAITI project. There doesn't appear to be a description of the actual project work anywhere here, but I do notice that some of these invoices are related to other clinics here in town."

Cassandra leaned over. "Let me take a look...I recognize

that one. It's a small clinic in a bad part of town, receiving lots of money for unspecified 'equipment'. That is strange."

"What's strange?"

"That place is notorious for being understaffed and not having enough equipment."

Fabi shrugged. "Maybe he used this project to change that?"

Cassandra continued to study the file. "You would think, except that I was there not too long ago for a meeting to show their data manager how to set up one of our databases, and believe me, they didn't have anything new that I could see."

Fabi studied the reports some more, finally shaking her head. "This seems irrefutable to me. The money is flowing their way for some sort of equipment. How much of the building did you see when you went there?"

"Not all of it, but I did see the patient areas. You would think that'd be the place for new equipment."

"Why don't we go over there and have a look?"

Cassandra looked unsure. "You mean set up a meeting—"

"No, I mean we go over there right now and see what's going on."

"Fabi, I don't know. For one thing, I don't have a key to that place."

Fabi grinned. "You're not going to let a little thing like that stop us, are you?"

The clinic lay on the outskirts of town, where there were no streetlights. Only a weak outer security bulb kept the place from being in complete darkness.

"Not the kind of place that shouts, 'all kinds of valuable stuff in here', is it?" Fabi whispered as she and Cassandra walked up to the entrance.

Cassandra shook her head. "I doubt anybody pays much attention to this place, including Dr. Avila. But we're here to find out, right?"

Fabi examined the latch on a window. "That's right,"

she said, reaching into her pocket and producing a nail file.

"Seriously, girl?" Cassandra sounded concerned.

"Just look around, make sure no one's coming. I'll have us in in a...got it!"

"Already?"

"Yeah, that was even easier than I thought." She pulled the window open, noting the lack of a screen. "Now I need a boost."

Cassandra held her hands together and interlaced her fingers so that Fabi could step on them. She boosted her up onto the window sill until Fabi could swing a leg over. A minute later, Fabi opened the front door and stuck her head out. "Come on in."

Cassandra entered the clinic and they closed and locked the door behind them. Not wanting the room lights to draw attention from outside, Fabi again relied upon her keychain flashlight. Cassandra led Fabi on a tour of the facility based on what she knew of the layout from previous visits, but it didn't take long.

"That's it?" Fabi asked, playing her beam along the walls.

"Told you this place isn't much, Fabi. Still not exactly sure what we're hoping to find, but…"

"Wait, hold on."

"Somebody coming?" Cassandra looked around.

"No, no. I mean, something's not right with this building—the building itself."

"Well yeah, it's old, dirty, falling apart in places, you can pick the windows open with a nail file..."

"No, that's not it, I mean look at this." She shone the flashlight on the far wall of the patient room in which they stood. "See how this wall ends here..."

"Uh, yeah?"

"Well, there's no way this wall corresponds to the outer wall of the building. When we were standing outside, we weren't just on the other side of this wall right here, we had to be at least another ten feet away."

Cassandra shook her head. "Fabi, building codes here

are not what they are in the states. It's anything goes. No permits, no licensing, nothing."

"No way this wall here matches up with the outer dimensions. So what's in the space in between?"

Cassandra threw her arms up. "Wild animals, probably. Spiders. Who cares?"

Fabi paused the flashlight beam on a bookshelf containing procedural manuals against the wall, and now she walked to it. She shone the beam behind the case, up to the ceiling and back down. Then, while Cassandra continued to question her sanity, she pulled on one end of the bookcase. The bookcase swung toward her, eliciting a gasp from Cassandra.

"Told ya." Behind the bookcase was a door.

"That door is locked, though, and this one doesn't look like your nail file is going to do it."

They examined the door lock. An electronic, alphanumeric keypad was embedded in the metal door. A green LED in one corner of the keypad indicated it had power. Fabi traced the outline of the door with her light and saw that her coworker was right. This was a serious piece of construction; the only way in was through that keypad. She put the light beam on it while considering the possibilities.

Cassandra shook her head. "Oh no. I see your wheels turning, girl. Don't even think about it. If you get the code wrong too many times, an alarm could go off."

"One try. Just give me one try..." She was staring intently at the keypad, the keys labeled 1, with ABC, 2, DEF...

"What, you're just going to put in some random numbers?"

"Definitely not. This thing is letters and numbers. Let's go with some kind of code word that would be easy to remember. That's how most people set up passwords."

"Okay, so what's the password?"

"Well, unless you have a better idea, I can only think of one that makes any sense: the project name."

Cassandra's eyes widened. "HAITI?"

Fabi moved her finger carefully across the keypad, depressing the key corresponding to each letter of the name. An LED flashed red each time she pressed a button. "...T...I...Enter."

The keypad LED flashed yellow and then went to a steady green. They heard no sound of any kind, but Fabi pushed on the door and sucked in her breath as it swung inward, into a new room.

Deciding that since it was contained within the outer and inner walls of the building, it was safe to turn overhead lights on, Fabi flipped up the light switch she found next to the door. Racks of fluorescent tube lighting flickered to life on the ceiling.

Cassandra could not stifle a gasp. "Oh my God."

Clearly, they were now in a laboratory of some sophistication. Lab benches supporting modern instruments such as computers, stereomicroscopes, centrifuges and spectrophotometers ran wall-to-wall. Fabi turned to look at her friend.

"Looks like this little clinic isn't so small after all. Now you tell me...why would Dr. Avila want to hide all this?"

Cassandra looked around the room. "I have no idea just by looking at this stuff what he's up to in here."

But Fabi was already in motion, heading toward one end of the lab. "I have a feeling this lab isn't the only hidden room. I'm betting this concealed space follows the entire perimeter of the building, between the outer building wall and the inner room wall. Let's check it out."

"Sure, why not? That attitude hasn't gotten us into any trouble so far..." Cassandra followed Fabi to the end of the lab. Sure enough, Fabi turned the corner and walked into another space hidden between walls.

Although the overhead lights weren't on in this section yet, there was light emanating from a series of plant grow lights suspended from the ceiling but hanging low over a bed of fern-like plants.

"Now this is just plain weird." Fabi made eye contact with Cassandra. "Tell me, what does growing plants have to do with running a health clinic?"

Cassandra shrugged and shook her head. "Certain kinds of plants might have some purpose, if you get my drift, but ferns? I have no idea. Fabi, listen, maybe we should go. We've seen more than enough to know something is going on. We can think about how to bring it up with Dr. Avila on Monday."

"Let me just see what's around this corner here and then we'll go, all right?"

Reluctantly, Cassandra followed Fabi into the new area. This one was dimly lit with nightlight-style bulbs, but it was enough to see that they had entered a patient care area. Two rows of cots were lined up in the center of the room, with people dozing on each of them.

"What *is* this? This is not an area suitable for housing patients." Cassandra sounded livid. She moved about the cots. "And look: these people are restrained!"

"These over here, too. They all are," Fabi confirmed.

"Oh my God! I recognize this one. This is a former patient of mine." She went to the cot and stooped to get a better look at the woman, a local Haitian of middle age. Fabi joined her friend at the cot as she attempted to wake the patient.

"Mrs. Rameau? It's me, Cassandra Damas. Wake up, please."

The woman stirred against her restraints—both wrists and ankles secured with thick leather cuffs to the frame of the bed.

"Why do you think they have her restrained?" Fabi wondered.

"Sometimes it's done to protect the patient from themselves, but I've never known Mrs. Rameau to be that way. Plus, *all* of the patients here are restrained."

Suddenly Mrs. Rameau bent at the waist and sat bolt upright. Her eyes opened wide and she leaned in to Cassandra.

"It's okay, Mrs. Rameau, I'm here to help you."

The patient thrust her head at Cassandra's arm. She

pulled away just as Rameau's teeth snapped hard shut.

"Calm down please, Mrs. Rameau. I'm only trying to help. How long have you been here? What is this place?"

But the woman only snarled and growled in return. "Something is definitely not right with her, Cassandra. She looks really out of it. And her skin, it looks really weird."

"Really weird? Is that your professional medical opinion?" Clearly, Cassandra took offense at something negative being said about her patient.

"I'm sorry, I don't mean anything personal by it."

Suddenly they heard the sound of a car engine approaching outside. Cassandra pointed back the way they had come. "We should get out of here." She tried to ease the patient back onto the cot, speaking soothing words to her, but the woman was in a frenzy, non-responsive and thrashing around.

They moved as fast as they could without bumping into things through the patient area and back into the plant lab. Fabi eyed the strange ferns, fluorescing odd colors as she passed through into the lab stocked with equipment. There was a computer in here, and Fabi lit it up to check for an Internet connection. Dial-up, a very slow connection, but a connection nonetheless. She began to type.

Cassandra was impatient. "What are you *doing*? Let's go."

"Sending Maddock and Bones an email with what we've seen. We'll have to go to the police, I'm afraid, but I want him to know. Just in case..."

"You mention him a lot. Did you know that?"

Fabi ignored her. She typed out a few cursory lines. "Okay, good enough." She clicked the Send button. "Let's skedaddle!"

She snapped the email window closed and flipped off the machine.

The pair of coworkers moved through the lab until they reached the hidden bookcase entrance. They exited into the clinic proper and then Fabi shut the keycoded door and swung the bookcase back into place. Moving through the clinic as quickly as they could with all lights off, even the flashlight, they came to the front door. Cassandra peeked through a window.

"Car's parked out front now!"

"See anyone?"

"No, no one's in it."

Fabi put her hand on the door. "Let's go."

Cassandra nodded and the two women stepped outside. No sooner did Fabi turn around to close the front door than Cassandra shouted, "Look…" But that was all she got out before a strong hand covered her mouth. A black man wearing a white lab coat threw Cassandra hard onto the ground.

Fabi, meanwhile, had taken stock of the situation and backed up enough to assume a fighting stance. She feigned a kick and the man smiled, thinking she was faking it. He moved in. Fabi spun around and closed with a foot to the man's throat that dropped him instantly.

"You recognize him?" Fabi panted as the man lay gasping.

Cassandra shook her head. "I recognize we should go."

With that, the two ran off into the night. When they had made it a safe distance away and it was clear no one else was pursuing them, Cassandra turned to Fabi while they walked toward their car.

"Remind me never to piss you off, by the way. I'll never make you wait to use the printer again, I promise. I had no idea you could fight like that."

Fabi smiled. "I was in the Navy for a bunch of years. It's where I met Bones."

"Ah, so I take it Bones is a fighter, then, too."

"He's a terrific guy. But let's just say you don't want to get on his bad side. Cassandra, look out!"

A van, headlights out, came around a curve in the road. The side door slid open and four men, their faces concealed, leapt out. Cassandra never had time to complete her sentence before the two women were desperately fighting off the new arrivals. A single man quickly subdued

Cassandra, leaving Fabi to take on the other three. The ex-Navy girl held her own at first, landing some crisp punches, but she soon found herself overwhelmed by the sheer weight of superior size and numbers.

"What do you want?" Maybe she could reason with them, talk her way out of this. At first she had been concerned this was a random violent crime, perhaps even attempted sexual assault, but combined with the events inside the clinic and the strange happenings surrounding her cousin's death, she wasn't so sure.

While the three men held her, the fourth approached her slowly. "Maybe we can solve this right now. Answer one question for me, and we will let you and your friend go." He jerked a thumb back at the van, where Cassandra's muffled cries now emanated.

Fabi didn't hesitate. "Okay. What is it?"

"Where is the treasure?"

A chill coursed through Fabi's veins as the full extent of what she had gotten herself into with this treasure hunt slugged her like a fist to the gut. Immediately she feared not only for herself and Cassandra, who was especially innocent, but also for Bones, Maddock and Willis. She should have made it more clear that the locals would be more interested in the treasure, and more vicious when it came to going after it.

"What treasure?"

"Please do not waste my time. The treasure your cousin sought."

Fabi saw there was no use in prevaricating.

"I have no idea!" She hoped the truth in the statement would add to the conviction in her voice. But with the ringleader's next words that hope was destroyed. He addressed his men while walking away.

"Throw her in the van."

Chapter 29

Off the coast of Alto Velo Island

Bones stretched and yawned as he stared at the electronic display for the device they towed behind the *Sea Foam* that would signal them when they had found metal on the seafloor.

"Tired of 'mowing the lawn'." The phrase was a reference to the fact that the boat was running back and forth in a grid pattern in long, predictable swaths as it dragged the instrumentation behind it, searching for the proverbial needle in a haystack. Hundreds, thousands of square miles of ocean to search for a near pinpoint deposit of gold and silver coins, although the ship's cannons and cannonballs could be a telltale giveaway, too.

Maddock turned the wheel as he brought the vessel into yet another U-turn to begin searching down a new lane. Willis exhaled heavily as he eyeballed the magnetometer monitor while Bones watched the sidescan sonar. "Can't we just hire some nerd to watch the screens?"

Maddock eased the boat into its new lane and looked over at his friend. "Tell you what. If we find this treasure, we'll hire one, okay?"

This seemed to satisfy Willis and Bones as well, both of whom went back to monitoring the instrument displays without further complaint. Time marched on, however, and as Maddock watched the needle on the fuel gauge slowly lean to the left, he began to wonder himself if they should call it a day. He was about to suggest one more leg to drag the instrument package when Bones let out a holler.

"Hold up! Got something here."

Maddock slowed the boat. Bones' eyes were still riveted to the display. "Right here! Take a look."

Maddock saw Willis' eyes bug out as he checked Bones'

screen before quickly moving back to his own. Maddock eyed the dense array of shadow lines on the screen, and then concentrated on the region Bones' finger pointed to. Sure enough, an easily discernible anomaly interrupted the repeating pattern.

"What's it look like for you, Willis?" Maddock took a look at the magnetometer readout, and it, too, signaled the presence of something unusual—and metallic—in the seabed below their hull.

"What's our depth?" Maddock asked.

Bones eyed his screen again. "Ninety feet."

"That's divable!" Maddock jumped back to the helm, cut the engines and hit the switch to drop anchor.

The three of them donned their scuba gear and took a careful look at the waters around the boat to make certain they were still alone. Satisfied they were working unobserved, the trio moved onto a dive platform that hung off the boat's stern.

Splashing into the sea, Maddock, Bones and Willis descended through the clear blue water. The bottom was already visible even though they still had seventy feet to go to reach it. A dense school of silver fish parted beneath them as they made their way down feet first. Beams of sunlight sparkled and shifted around them. Looking up, the *Sea Foam*'s hull was clearly visible as a dark oblong shape outlined against the light background of sunlit surface water. Below, the dark topography of the seafloor beckoned with the promise of hidden treasure.

The sophisticated equipment on board their boat was of no practical use to them down here. All it could do was point them in the right direction, and then it was up to them to do the legwork for the rest of the way. That didn't mean they had no technological help, though. Both Bones and Willis carried underwater metal detectors. By passing the unit's disc directly over the seafloor, if metal was not too far beneath, an audible signal would sound in the gadget's headphones.

Upon reaching the bottom, which was mostly flat and

sandy, the trio of divers checked their gauges to confirm depth and remaining tank air. Satisfied the numbers were in their favor, they went to work. Maddock operated unencumbered, relying on his vision to scan the area for bigger picture clues, while Bones and Willis swam slowly, scouring the bottom by sweeping their metal detectors back and forth, listening for telltale signals of buried metal.

What had appeared on the screens aboard the *Sea Foam* as a significant metallic feature looked like nothing of the sort now that the ex-SEALs were down here. Maddock laid his eyes on only sand and seaweed. It was not lost on him that it was possible, after centuries' worth of storms and shifting sands, that a shipwreck could be buried many feet below the bottom, making it unsalvageable for all practical intents and purposes. Knowing there was nothing he could do about that, he continued to survey the area, looking for anything that might signal the remains of a wreck.

He was finning his way across the search area when he heard a sharp pinging sound—a noise he had paid attention to many times before. Either Bones or Willis was signaling by banging a dive knife against their aluminum air tank. Maddock spun around to see Willis look up from swinging his detector, also searching for the source of the noise. Maddock continued his slow spin until he caught sight of Bones, looking his way and waving an arm.

He and Willis swam fast over to Bones. The tall Indian had already set his detector aside and was now digging into the bottom with a metal scoop. Willis, who also carried one, joined Bones in the digging effort while Maddock kept overwatch, on the lookout for marine predators, or worse. He'd heard plenty of stories of treasure divers being accosted underwater by less than welcoming locals who would rather have the treasure for themselves once the hard work of locating it had been done.

Clouds of silt made it hard to see as the hole in the seabed deepened. Bones raised a hand for Willis to stop digging, and then both men started fanning the water with their gloved hands, attempting to clear the area of the suspended particles that made it hard to see what was in the hole. After a couple of minutes of this effort, Bones stuck a hand down into the excavation. He pushed his facemask into it, closely examining what lay on the bottom. Suddenly he retracted his arm from the depression and held it high.

Sunbeams seemed to reflect from his fingers, radiating in all directions as Maddock realized what Bones held. He swam to the Cherokee and peered at the object clutched between his fingers.

A gold coin.

Bones held it out in front of Maddock's mask. The coin had some corrosion, but they could still make out a bust on one side and a shield on the other. Maddock grinned and gave Bones the "okay" sign before dropping the gold piece into an artifact bag he had clipped to his weight belt.

Willis, who had begun searching the small pit while Bones showed Maddock his find, also emerged holding a treasure. Another gold coin similar to the first. Maddock added it to his pouch and then looked on while Bones and Willis went back to the excavation. After a few minutes of searching, including passing the metal detectors over the bottom of the pit, it became clear that their honey hole had run dry.

Maddock gave hand signals to indicate they should search the rest of the area. The three of them fanned out again over the sand, but after combing the site until their air supplies were low, Maddock jerked a thumb toward the surface, and they began their ascent back to the boat.

Back aboard the *Sea Foam*, Maddock, Bones and Willis shrugged out of their dive gear and decided to search the narrower area in the vicinity of the dive site for larger signatures on the magnetometer and sidescan sonar. Maddock got behind the wheel and had just cranked up the engine when he noticed his mobile phone blinking to indicate he had a new message.

He gave the wheel over to Bones, leaving Willis to monitor the instrument displays while Maddock checked his message.

A new email from Fabi caught his eye. His eyes narrowed as he read the text.

"Bones, Maddock: I've been doing some digging around the clinic and found something crazy. Looks like Dr. Avila is up to something bad. I think he's behind the zombie attacks. Gotta get out of here. More later."

Concern swept over Maddock's features as he pondered Fabi's email. Was she onto something or simply spooked? Right now he couldn't be entirely sure, but given everything that was going on, it was nothing to downplay.

"Hey Bones, Fabi sent us an email."

The Indian looked over from the wheel. "Sent *us* an email? You mean, me?"

"Shut up and listen, this is serious. She says—"

Willis' husky voice interrupted them both. "Whoa, I got something here. Something interesting."

Chapter 30

"Check the sonar image, here." Willis pointed to a display where a field of hazy gray was plainly visible in a jagged black rip. Maddock and Bones crowded around to get a look.

Maddock shook his head. "That can't be metal."

Bones ran a fingertip along the shape of the intrusive outline. "It's not metal, it's a geological feature. Part of the bottom."

Willis nodded. "Some kind of trench, or crevasse. But look: I think there's something down there, some open space near the bottom. See this?" He stabbed a pointer finger on the lower left end of the unusual feature, where a subtle splotch of discoloration could be seen.

Bones appeared concerned. "How deep is that?"

Willis shook his head slowly. "Hard to say. It's a narrow gorge type deal, and we're not positioned exactly over it, so it's reading the bottom around it. But if I had to guess, I'd say at least one hundred feet." A doubtful look took over his features before adding, "Currents are going to be a bear down there, too. Looks dicey, from a diver standpoint."

Bones looked away from the screen, making eye contact with Maddock and Willis. "How could a Spanish treasure ship, which was over a hundred feet long, have ended up down in that narrow crevasse?"

Willis wagged a finger back and forth over the gray hazy part of the display that surrounded the more distinct feature of the gorge. "I'm no geologist, but after looking at a lot of these readings in the service, I'd say it looks like there's been a shifting of rock sometime in the past." He paused, shrugged, and then went on. "It could be that seismic activity caused it, but it's a pretty safe bet that it was probably a much larger space in the past. Whatever it was that caused it, the whole place looks like it could collapse at pretty much any time, and I'm not looking forward to going down there if that's part of the plan."

Maddock clapped Willis on the back. "Don't worry. It's like playing Jenga. Keep a steady hand and you'll be fine. Let's get suited up."

Willis took a last look at the sonar display and then reluctantly left the console. Bones sat there, however, a worried look on his face. Maddock addressed him. "What, you're scared, too?"

Bones shook his head. "Scared I'm partnered with such a geek. *Jenga*? Really? Who are you, Maddock?"

With that, Bones headed for the dive platform.

Willis let Maddock and Bones take the first dive, citing the need for someone to keep an eye on the boat and the sonar readings. Maddock wondered if the unstable passageway gave his friend pause, but he didn't give Willis any hassle about it. Deep diving was serious business, and if someone felt like they shouldn't do a dive, then they probably shouldn't.

Maddock pulled on a fin and looked up at Willis. "Not a bad idea. By the looks of it, three might be a crowd down there in that tight space, anyway."

"Be safe down there. We're a long way from help." Willis looked around, the desolate island of Alto Velo their only landscape. Then he added, "While you're down there, I'll put together a couple of extra scuba rigs and leave them hanging down at twenty feet so you have extra air for your decompression stop if you need it."

Maddock and Bones splashed into the water and swam to the boat's anchor line. They waved to Willis and submerged, gripping the rope with one hand as they followed its length down to the bottom. When they were within sight of the boat's anchor, they could see right away that there was indeed a large opening in the seafloor.

The duo swam over the flat portion of seafloor, which looked much like that of their previous dive site, until the bottom began to slope sharply downward. They paused, kneeling on the bottom before the incline became too steep, staring down into a dark abyss. Across the chasm, perhaps forty feet away, the seafloor resumed its flat pattern. At this point, as they scrambled for their dive lights in order to see into the trench, neither of them could blame Willis for wanting to mind the boat.

Maddock bumped into Bones by accident, swayed by a powerful current that ripped across the opening of the chasm. Bones gave him a rude gesture and Maddock pointed down. *Let's go before we get swept away from the site.*

They let more air out of their buoyancy compensator vests in order to sink into the crevasse, dropping straight down into it and avoiding contact with the sides, which could cloud the water and make it difficult to see. Playing their light beams around the walls of the chasm as they descended, Maddock and Bones could see colorful sponges and sea anemones. A large crab scuttled out of the cone of light that had invaded its dim home, and a school of small, pink fish darted this way and that.

Maddock and Bones stayed close together as they dropped, not knowing what to expect, if the chasm would branch off at some point, or how deep it would get. If they needed to communicate, they wanted to be able to do so immediately without having to swim to their dive buddy. Maddock was pointing to his depth gauge, expressing concern that it might get too deep before they could safely reach bottom, when suddenly the rocky slope grew less steep as it branched off to their right.

They followed it, swimming with careful fin strokes into the gloom. As they passed through a tunnel, Maddock shone his light ahead, noticing with excitement that the passage branched out into a labyrinth of small caves and various tunnels. That was when the rock passageway in which they swam started to move. Maddock was alerted to it at first by the sound of rock grating on rock. Then he saw Bones' head on a swivel, looking all around for the source of the sound.

Bones pointed up, high on the tunnel wall, and Maddock saw the rock that made up the tunnel shift. As he watched, it stopped, but the small cloud of rock dust now floating in the water over their heads told him that this was not a stable place, and not a safe one, either. Maddock made hand signals for Bones that asked him if he wanted to call the dive and head back to the boat.

The determined man shook his head and motioned forward. He and Maddock swam on, eventually coming to a fork in the passage. Maddock aimed his light down the new fork but inside saw only a chaotic jumble of precariously stacked boulders. He advised Bones to avoid the fork and continue ahead toward what appeared to be a cavern.

Upon reaching the end of the passage, they were confronted with a crumbling stone archway in the end of the tunnel. Not sure whether it was a natural formation or a manmade one, Maddock hesitated to pass beneath it, concerned about causing a cave-in. He looked through the archway to see if it was worth passing through at all, but within seconds Bones shot through the opening into the new space. Maddock was forced to follow—he could not leave his partner, dive buddy and friend behind no matter what.

Maddock consulted his air pressure gauge. Low. Enough air to get back to the surface, but not a whole lot more than that. He was glad now that Willis was setting up the extra decompression tanks. He tapped Bones on the shoulder and let him know they should turn back soon. They'd explored in and out of dozens of tunnels and caves so far, but found nothing promising. Sometimes the technology plays tricks, Maddock thought. There really was no substitute for actually being somewhere in person, and right now that presence was allowing him to see that there was nothing worth—

Bones' frantically waving hand arrested Maddock's attention. He swam the short distance to his dive buddy and found him waist deep in a small, rocky depression in the cave floor. Maddock had just settled in to wait for Bones to hopefully pull something out of there when the Indian backed out of the hole and turned around to face Maddock, shaking his head.

Still empty handed. Maddock tapped Bones on the arm to remind him it was time to leave. He angled his body to be able to fit out through a rocky chute. As he turned to maneuver, the sleek shape of a blue shark rocketed past him, deeper into the cave. As he tracked it carefully, arcing into a turn, his gaze caught on something pale on the cave floor below him and to his right. The shark disappeared through a tunnel, leaving Maddock to ponder what he was looking at. Deciding the only object he'd seen thus far that wasn't part of the rocks making up the tunnels was worth checking out, he dropped down to the bottom.

Bones' shadowy form passed over him on the way out, and Maddock knew his friend was looking down, wondering what he was doing, if he had found something. And there it was: a whitish round object, partially buried in sand. Maddock closed his fist around it and pulled. He was not prepared for the fit of revulsion he felt when he realized he had grabbed hold of a skull.

A human skull.

A significant crack ran nearly the length of it from right eye socket to the back. Whether caused in some long ago battle, or not so long ago, for that matter, or if the trauma was a result of lying on the seafloor for hundreds of years, Maddock could not tell. He saw Bones' light land on the macabre find and he turned the skull to face him briefly with its unsettling perma-grin before setting it back where he had found it.

As he did so, he let his dive light dangle by the wrist strap so that it bobbed around randomly while he handled the skull. He was just about to grip the light again when he saw a glint of golden light off in a shadowy corner.

Quickly, knowing his air supply was being dangerously depleted by every breath, Maddock pushed off the bottom, keeping his light aimed at the mysterious corner. Before he even reached the pinpoint source of the reflection, he could see that he had found something remarkable.

A section of wooden planks jutted up from a grouping

of boulders. Maddock played his light around the wood and realized with a start that he was looking at the remains of a ship. He examined the area in more detail and found more wreckage, and more reflections from the sandy portion of the cave floor. Sifting a hand through the sand, his fingers came up clutching two Spanish silver *reals*. He tapped his knife on his tank and waved his light in Bones' direction to alert him to the find.

Moments later the big Indian was at his side, also sifting through the sand and bagging silver, as well as gold, coins. In addition to coins, though, Bones also uncovered a palm-sized jeweled cross, laden with emeralds. He shined his light on it to show Maddock before dropping it into his bag.

Maddock carefully inspected the seafloor and bagged various finds along with Bones—mostly Spanish *reals*, but also the occasional artifact, such as a silver cup and a length of gold chain. Visions of newfound wealth dancing through his head, the ex-SEAL had to force himself to control his breathing, to stay calm and rational.

Thinking he had time for one last artifact before absolutely needing to leave for the boat, Maddock brushed the sand off of a gray metal object that was relatively flat. Brushing aside a little more sand, he could see that he had found the breastplate of a Spanish warrior. He was not a historian, but it seemed commensurate with the same period as that of the coins—early 1700s.

Maddock was debating whether he should leave the sizable object in place and come back for it later along with the rest of the treasure that still lay about here, when he felt a rush of water next to his left ear, and then a metal dart slammed into the breastplate with an audible *tink*.

Aside from the fact that this projectile had missed his head by maybe an inch, the first thing that registered in Maddock's brain was the word, *flechette*. It was an odd word, but one he knew because of his SEAL training. As underwater warriors, they had been trained in the use of an assortment of deadly weapons suitable for marine use while SCUBA diving. One of these was a specialized type of gun, made for underwater use that fired a small dart called a *flechette*. He still recalled his arms school instructor in the SEALs introducing the weapon to him and his class. The metal darts, with a short shank and flared tip, had originally been dropped from aircraft by the hundreds on ground troops in World War I.

But these thoughts were but a flash in Maddock's now activated brain, a mind that had been trained not to react with panic when facing danger. And right now, he and Bones were clearly in danger, for someone else had come for the treasure they had found.

Chapter 31

Maddock recognized the underwater pistol now pointed at his head as a Russian SPP-1. This understanding didn't slow him down, though, but was something he knew instantly as soon as he looked at the weapon. Knowing it was more powerful than a spear gun, but inaccurate, Maddock reacted immediately, grabbing the old breastplate from the sand on which he knelt. He raised it just as the second *flechette*, a five-inch steel dart, struck the breastplate.

Maddock heard the same sound as before when the dart struck his impromptu shield. He took a chance and leaned right, still holding the fragmented breastplate out in front of him, and finned his way behind a cluster of rocks, using them as cover. But another round was not fired. Maddock guessed his assailant was taking his time with the next shot. The ex-SEAL knew the SPP-1 only carried four rounds, and two of them had already been discharged.

Behind his cover, Maddock doused his lights and grabbed a knife from the sheath worn inside his left calf. Looking over to his right, he saw Bones cut his lights as well.

Maddock recognized a new problem now, in the form of the attacker's dive partner. A second man, also armed with an underwater pistol, swam toward Bones. *Four more rounds, total of six left now,* Maddock calculated.

But he knew that Bones could take care of himself, and right now Maddock had his own problems to worry about. He remained stock still behind his rocky cover as the intruder who had been stalking him approached Maddock's hiding spot. The man moved in, pistol held in the ready position.

As the attacker rounded the corner of Maddock's cover, finger squeezing the trigger of his SPP-1, Maddock flung the breastplate up to stop the next shot while simultaneously slashing with his dive knife. He caught his foe's gun hand with the blade, releasing a puffy cloud of blood—appearing black at this depth—into the water. The would-be killer yanked his wounded hand back, dropping the gun in the process.

Maddock sprang off the bottom and cracked his bleeding assailant across the mask with the piece of breastplate. The mask splintered into a spiderweb of cracks, effectively blinding the man. The man flailed his arms about wildly, attempting to fend off a death blow he feared was coming, but Maddock instead retreated back behind cover and watched for the second man.

He expected to see him closing in on Bones, but Maddock was surprised to see no one at all where Bones had been moments before. Suddenly he felt the currents change ever so slightly, little more than a sensation of cold water moving against his neck where before all had been calm. But it was enough to make him spin around in time to see the enemy diver about to shoot Maddock in the back with a pistol.

Maddock started to bring his shield up but he knew he would not be fast enough. He tightened his stomach muscles against the assault of the *flechette* he knew was coming, but at that moment Bones' towering form appeared behind the shooter. Bones' lights were still off, and Maddock avoided signaling him so as not to give away his presence. The big Indian's hand came down over the shooter's head from behind and ripped off his mask, tossing it aside.

Both assailants now incapacitated, Maddock grabbed Bones by the shoulder and pointed up toward the tunnel that led out. He didn't even look at his air pressure gauge, but knew they were perilously low and had to get out now. Maddock thought about turning on his light and looking around for the guns, but decided he didn't have time for any further confrontation.

He and Bones swam fast through the cavern to the tunnel by which they had arrived. Forced to swim single file through the narrow chute, Bones went first, Maddock close on his fin tips. About halfway through the chute, which angled upward at a forty-five degree angle, Maddock saw light playing on the rocky walls. His own lights were still off, and he thought that Bones may have flipped his on, but then he saw his friend turn to look back, clearly wondering if Maddock had turned his lights on.

Maddock whipped his head around to look behind them. Entering the chute was one of the divers they had dispatched. Maddock cursed himself for not thinking to grab the still intact face mask they'd ripped off the one diver and left on the bottom. Not to mention the guns. Maddock frantically pointed forward and kicked, ushering Bones on through the chute. The passageway curved left and as they followed it, another flechette zipped past both of them and slammed into the tunnel wall.

Again, Maddock picked up the pace, shoving Bones ahead of them as they sought to elude their armed pursuer. Even as he expended additional energy, Maddock made it a point not to breathe faster or heavier, knowing his air supply was extremely low.

They reached another bend and as they rounded it, this time Maddock felt a sharp pain in his thigh. He stopped moving in order to assess the hit. Fortunately the flechette had struck him at an angle, so that it did not penetrate deeply. He tried to keep moving but the water pushing against it caused it to wiggle painfully in his leg, so he paused to rip it out. He flipped on his headlamp to examine the spent round in order to make sure it was still intact, that a piece of it hadn't broken off inside his leg. He dropped it and pushed forward.

Bones had stopped up ahead, looking back, wondering why Maddock had fallen so far behind. Maddock waved him on. No need to endanger both of their lives. He'd rather have one of them make it back to Willis to tell what happened down here than to have both of them die, either by physical attack or by running out of air. Bones kicked off toward the chute exit while Maddock pressed on. He was now considerably slower than the naturally speedy Bones due to his leg injury, but still managed to make decent forward progress.

Up ahead, the archway that marked the entrance to the chasm shipwreck area loomed. As Maddock kicked toward it, he recalled how unstable it was, the rocks that comprised it shifting and moving when he and Bones had passed through. An idea was forming in his brain when a flechette grazed his wetsuit, tearing it and skinning the flesh, but this time not embedding into his body. He continued swimming toward the archway, the idea coalescing into an action-plan by the time he reached it.

Maddock unsheathed his knife. As he passed underneath the precarious arch, he began hacking at some of the loose stones at the base of the archway. He pried several of them loose, keeping an eye on a massive boulder overhead, which wobbled, but held in place. He now saw two dive lights illuminating him and his immediate surroundings. He supposed both divers had now reached him, even though one had only a cracked mask. Wincing as he moved his leg in order to wedge his blade beneath a large rock, he knew he needed to make something happen unless he wanted to end up as a flechette pincushion.

Maddock kept at it, knowing the rocks would topple soon. What he wasn't so sure of was which way they would fall. Hopefully not on top of him, but it was a chance he had to take. With a precious normal breath rather than the shallow ones he'd been taking in order to conserve air, he put all of his strength into moving one of the archway's foundation stones. Right hand on his makeshift pry bar, left on the rock itself, he heaved with everything he had, grunting into his mouthpiece with the effort.

He felt something slide and then, with a final shove, Maddock looked up to see the towering archway start to collapse. The rocks making up the sides tumbled out of place first, then the top. They fell slower in water than if they had been on land, but people moved slower underwater, too, and Maddock was under no illusion as to his fate should one of these rocks land on him.

He registered the chaotic movement of his pursuers' lights, their beams dancing around the falling archway. Seeing the boulders piling up and choking off the only entrance in or out of the treasure chasm, Maddock knew he had mere seconds to make it through the archway. Apparently the competing treasure hunters had come to the same decision, as they no longer held their weapons at the ready, but instead focused solely on swimming as fast as they could toward the archway portal.

Maddock spent no more time thinking things through. He powered through the arch just as the last open gaps were filled in by a cascade of tumbling boulders, the unnerving sound of heavy grating, rock-against-rock, filling the water all around him. His adrenaline spiked when he felt resistance as he tried to kick. He tugged his right leg and then realized the fin blade had been caught between two rocks, trapping it in between. He pulled hard but still could not free himself. At least his attackers had been walled off from him, stuck on the other side of the chasm. He figured they would probably find a way through; there were bound to be gaps here and there, but for the immediate future he was safe from that threat.

But any second he expected to inhale only to find there was nothing left to breathe. He had no time to be stuck. He considered simply removing the stuck fin and leaving it behind, but he would need all the propulsion he could get to make it back to the surface in time. Maddock brought his knife to the fin blade and sliced it off just above where it was pinned. The rubber separated easily and soon he had a stubby fin to work with on his right leg, like the kind body surfers wore. A lot better than nothing, Maddock thought, as he jetted off toward the surface.

Even though he felt a strong sense of elation at having eluded his pursuers and escaping the avalanche of his own making, Maddock still felt disappointment at having lost the bulk of the treasure. Other than the few pieces he and Bones now carried with them, the hoard was now blockaded behind the collapsed arch. It would be a massive undertaking to move significant loads of treasure through that heap of jumbled stones, essentially undoable, Maddock knew. The treasure was lost, and with it, his dreams.

He headed for the boat, the sounds of the still collapsing tunnel ringing hollow in his ears.

Chapter 32

Fabi felt the blindfold being roughly torn from her eyes. She did not recognize the man who tossed the fabric aside, though could tell he was a local Haitian of middle age, and had heard his associates call him by name: Odelin. She looked past her captor, trying to ascertain where she was. Inside, in what looked like the kitchen of a house, where she could hear but not see other men in the other rooms. Fabi sat on a chair, her hands tied behind her back but not to the chair itself, and her legs not bound. Looking sideways, she saw Cassandra in the same situation on a chair next to her.

"You." Odelin pointed at Fabi. "Up. Come with me." He waved toward the adjoining room. Fabi stood, and Cassandra began stammering. "F—Fabi? What's happening? What are they doing?"

Odelin stomped his boot on the wooden floor. "Silence, or you will be gagged."

"Don't worry, Cassandra. I'm right here. These men want something from me. When we get it sorted out, I'm sure they'll let us go like the gentlemen they are." She gave her captor a hard stare, but he only waved her on into the next room.

The dining room had once been nice, but had long since fallen into a state of neglect. The walls had cracks and spider webs dangled from corners. A table surrounded by mismatched chairs occupied the center of the smallish room, its surface cracked and dirty. Two other men waited in here, both standing against different walls and armed with submachine guns. These two still wore the concert T-shirts around their faces, Fabi noticed, but for some reason the one who led her in here, Odelin, was unconcerned about being masked. Would she recognize those holding the guns from around town?

She had little time to ponder this as Odelin shoved a

chair in front of her. He stood over her until she sat. Then he pushed her and her chair up to the table and walked around the table to sit opposite her. He stared at her.

"Fabiola Baptiste. Your cousin, David the priest, was looking for a shipwreck treasure thought to be here in the waters of Haiti."

"If you say so." Fabi struggled to keep her voice even, to keep her emotions in check. "I know nothing about what David was doing. I hadn't heard from him in months when he died. Perhaps you were responsible for his death?"

"Perhaps you will answer my questions without asking your own, or you will find that the ability to speak is a privilege afforded only to those who cooperate."

Fabi let her head loll back in frustration, speaking up to the ceiling. "I'm telling you, I don't know anything about a sunken treasure. I work in a medical clinic! What do I know about underwater treasure?"

"You have associates cooperating with you to find it. The Americans with a boat."

"They are acquaintances of mine from my old days in the American Navy. They are here on vacation to do some recreational scuba diving because I always told them what a beautiful and *hospitable* place Haiti was to visit."

Odelin shook his head slowly, taking on a pained expression as though saddened by what he had just heard. "Fabiola...I will ask you one more time. One Haitian to another. Where. Is. The. *Treasure*?"

"I'm sorry, but I'm running out of ways to say the same thing over and over. I don't know anything about any treasure, much less where it might be." She perked up as if receiving a new thought. "In the ocean. How about that? It's in the ocean."

Her captor appeared unfazed. "*Where* in the ocean?"

"I have no idea."

He looked to one of the men holding a gun and nodded. The guard promptly returned the nod without a word and left the room, leaving one armed man behind.

"We'll see about that."

Chapter 33

Off the coast of Alto Velo Island

Willis finished patching up Maddock's leg wound with *the Sea Foam*'s first aid kit. "You're good to go. In the future try to avoid pointy metal things."

Maddock shot him a look and picked up a pair of binoculars. He skulked about the deck of the *Sea Foam*, keeping watch for any approaching vessels that might signal reinforcements from their attackers. He scoured the sea in all directions, but so far they were alone on the ocean.

Bones had spread the contents of their treasure bags on a table and now gazed at the small assortment of pricey baubles, eyes glazing over as he imagined how much more they had to leave behind.

"Hey Maddock, you think there's any way we can get back through that archway you demolished to reach the rest of the treasure or what?"

Maddock let the binoculars drop around his neck as he, too, mentally relived the harrowing dive into the labyrinthine chasm. "Doesn't look too promising."

Bones looked up from the small amount of recovered treasures. "There's gotta be another way in there. Around that archway, or somewhere else, maybe?"

Discussion about whether or not the archway was the only way in or out of the treasure lair continued until Maddock's cellular phone rang. He picked it up and eyeballed the number on screen with curiosity.

Bones grinned. "Who is it? You finally find a female who wants to go out with you?"

Maddock shrugged. "Haiti number. Maybe it's Fabi." He raised his eyebrows at Bones before accepting the call and putting the phone to his ear.

But the new voice in his ear was male, and he was

surprised to recognize the name the caller identified himself as: Dr. Ricardo Avila. Maddock recalled Fabi mentioning him as the director of the local health clinics she worked for. Bones was making noise about letting him talk to "her" and Maddock almost missed it.

"Hold on. He says he has Fabi."

"Let me talk to her, will you?"

Maddock cupped his hand over the phone's microphone. "Bones," he hissed, "I don't mean *he has her* like he has her on the line, waiting to talk to us. I mean, he *has* her, as in, kidnapped, holding her prisoner. Let me talk."

Bones' expression darkened instantly and Willis stepped closer so as to overhear the call.

Maddock spoke into the phone. "Say again, please, Dr. Avila. I had some background noise. You are with Fabi?" He put the phone on speaker mode while Bones and Willis leaned in.

"Fabi is with me for now, Mr. Maddock. But her time is limited. I know what you and your friends are doing in Haiti with your boat."

"We came to console our friend and former Navy colleague, Fabi, after the death of her relative, and to do some diving while here."

"Diving for treasure, Mr. Maddock. Do not take me for a fool and try to make it sound as though you are on a routine vacation. You will listen to me now if you want to ever see Fabi again, is that clear?"

Bones nodded reflexively while Maddock responded. "Yes, that is clear Dr. Avila. Go ahead, I'm listening."

The voice carried a trace of the local island accent. *"In return for Fabiola's safe return, I want you to deliver me the treasure of the 1715 fleet."*

Maddock made no attempt to disguise his reactionary spitting sound. "With all due respect, Dr. Avila, that's ridiculous. I have no idea where that treasure is. If I did, I'd be a rich man on some megayacht in St. Martins or somewhere nice, not here on my old scow in dangerous places like Haiti." He waited for Avila to respond while eyeing the sunlight glinting off the table of treasures.

"No excuses, Mr. Maddock. Haiti is, as you say, a 'dangerous

place', and no one will bat an eye at the disappearance of yet another pretty girl. You have three days. You may reach me at the number you now have on your phone. If I do not have the bulk of that treasure in my possession in the next seventy-two hours, Fabi is a dead woman."

The connection clicked off and Maddock was left to stare at the phone screen while Bones and Willis stared at each other. At length, Maddock broke the stunned silence by pointing to the table that was sparsely covered with treasures. "You think he'd be happy with those?"

Bones shook his head while Willils said, "Probably just make him even meaner. He'd *know* we know where the treasure is if we show him those. You were telling him you have no idea."

Maddock nodded. "I thought that was the route that would give us the most options at this point. We could always tell him we found those later if we need to stall for more time. Like we're getting closer."

"What about actually getting the rest of it?" Bones stared over the boat's gunwale into the deep waters with an uncertain look on his face.

Maddock sighed heavily and shook his head. "Bones...there's just no way. Not in three days, anyhow. Not only has there been a collapse of the only known route into the treasure cave, but the place is already known to Avila's men, obviously. He just wants us to do all the work. He sent those divers after us. Those guys probably saw some of the same gold we did down there."

"If they survive to talk about it." Willis surveyed the waters around the boat. "I don't see any air bubbles coming up. We'd have seen them if they surfaced."

A grim moment of silence ensued after which Maddock said, "They probably have a vessel of some kind nearby, probably on the other side of Alto Velo somewhere, with at least one man on it. When and if the divers don't return, they'll assume we were behind it and then Avila will view this site with added significance."

Willis looked at Bones. "I know she means a whole lot to you, man, and I definitely don't want any harm to come to her either, but even without Avila's men down there, Maddock is right. It was unstable enough before he toppled that arch. Think of the operation it would be to clear a path back down there, excavate all that gold and get it back up. We're talking dozens of dives, if we can get through at all. I bet our decompression time alone would be a whole day if we added it all up."

Maddock nodded in silent agreement. "That doesn't mean there's nothing we can do, though."

Bones eyed him doubtfully. "Please don't say 'go to the cops'."

"I'm guessing Avila's got at least a few local law enforcement officers on his underground payroll," Willis added.

Maddock shook his head, his gray eyes hardening with resolve. "No cops. I'm talking about going after Fabi ourselves."

Chapter 34

Avila's island

"Looks nice enough." Bones shielded his eyes from the sun with a hand as he stood on the deck of the *Sea Foam* looking at a small island in the distance. Ringed with white sand beaches, the interior was elevated and covered in greenery, with a few towering palms poking through the top of the forest. It hadn't taken much research to locate this small island owned by the doctor. Located off Haiti's west coast in the Gulf of Gonâve, it was too small to appear on most maps, and when it did, no name was given for it.

"Looks can be deceiving." Willis squinted as he, too, took in the destination for their extraction mission while Maddock minded the helm.

"Yeah," Bones said, "I mean, take you as an example. You look like a big tough guy, but we all know in a fight I could take you down, no problem."

"Anytime you want to back that up, you let me know."

Maddock interrupted the verbal sparring. "All right, kids, I think this is as close as we can get to the island without attracting undue attention. We're going to have to swim it from here. Let's get the gear ready."

Maddock glanced up at the water's surface as he gripped the handles of his underwater scooter. A three-foot long torpedo-shaped craft, it ran silently on battery power and allowed the diver to cover long distances with minimal exertion. Bones and Willis flanked him on identical machines. Maddock saw the outline of palm trees through the water and knew they were very close to the beach. He looked for a cluster of boulders he'd seen in a satellite photo of Avila's island compound provided by Jimmy Letson. He found the cluster off to their right and turned toward it, the scooter dragging him effortlessly through the roiling water.

He sought the rocks because they protruded from the water, and that would provide cover, something to hide behind and shield them from anyone who might be looking as they broke the surface with their scooters. The trio reached them and by that point the water was so shallow they were barely concealed beneath it. Maddock popped his head up into the air and was relieved to find that the rocks did in fact block direct line of sight to the beach.

They waited there for a couple of minutes, listening while Willis faced out to sea, Bones watched to the left and Maddock to the right. After detecting nothing threatening, they ditched the scooters and the scuba gear out of sight on the bottom and walked around the rocks.

Willis grinned widely as they made their way. "Just like old times."

Bones said, "This isn't what I expected when you told me we'd be treasure hunting, Maddock." But his smile said that he relished the excitement, even the danger.

Maddock held a hand up and they crouched there a moment, knowing from Jimmy's intel that Avila's stronghold would not be unguarded. Sure enough, they eyed a guard armed with some type of long gun, probably an automatic rifle, walking the edge of the beach where it met the forest.

"A single guard?" Willis shook his head slowly as though he could not believe it.

Maddock pointed to the middle of the island, where the elevation was highest. "Don't think this will be the only one. This is just the perimeter detail. The main house will be heavily patrolled."

They waited patiently for the guard to pass by their position and make his way further down the edge of the beach. Then the trio of amphibious warriors dashed across the beach to the outer perimeter of Avila's compound, where a rusty barbed wire fence blocked the way through the forest. While Bones made short work of a section of fence with a folding multi-tool, Maddock's gaze went higher, scanning the trees.

"See something?" Willis whispered while he watched the guard walk far down the beach. "Guard's gonna turn back this way soon."

Maddock pointed about fifty feet to their left, where a break in the foliage—either a very wide path or a narrow clearing—offered obvious transit through the bush. But then he raised his finger, moving it up from the same spot, where a boxy object was just visible high on the trunk of a coconut palm tree.

"Camera. We'll have to cut through the dense foliage." Maddock pointed into the jungle, where the closely spaced trees would shield them from the camera's lens.

"Keep our eyes open for more, too." Willis' gaze travelled through the rain forest canopy, seeking additional optics, but finding none. "Clear as far as I can see, which isn't far."

Maddock signaled they should move out and the three of them crept into the greenery. The trio moved with a high degree of stealth, avoiding loud footfalls. They were sneaky to the point that small animals were occasionally startled by their seemingly sudden appearance, birds and rodents retreating hastily.

After covering nearly half a mile, Bones, who had taken Maddock's right flank, held up a hand. Willis and Maddock eyed him expectantly. "Hold on," came his whispered reply. Suddenly Maddock understood why Bones was feeling on edge.

"It's awfully quiet, isn't it?"

Bones nodded. "Too quiet."

Suddenly a face peeked out from the foliage above their heads and Bones pointed it out. Two intelligent eyes stared at them, but they weren't human. A monkey. It dangled by its hands and swung to another branch, giving them a good look at the whole body. A large primate, nearly as tall as Bones, its fur was black and white, with bright blue eyes, making for a striking appearance against the green canopy.

"Weird." Bones watched the animal hang from its new

branch. "Weren't we just talking about how monkeys went extinct in Haiti hundreds of years ago? And now here are some more—different kind—on a different island."

Willis shrugged. "I guess they came back."

Maddock advised they should just keep moving. They started out again through the underbrush, but then the creature dropped onto Bones. "What the heck is it with me and these things?" He panted as he contorted and gyrated in an attempt to throw the beast from his body. Willis helped pry its arms loose from the bear hug it had around Bones' midsection, and then Bones was able to spin away from it, leaving it to stand on the forest floor in the middle of the three men, eyes level with them.

"Three to one, baboon boy, get outta here!" But it seemed Willis' taunt served only to threaten the monkey, for it charged at Maddock, who threw a right cross at it only to have the monkey block it with its left forearm. Bones stepped up and kicked it aside with a well-placed right boot. The monkey, similar to a Capuchin, but much larger, staggered backward yet held its ground. It sprang toward the three humans again. This time, Bones, knowing that suffering a solid blow to the head could be fatal, took decisive action.

He removed his dive knife from the sheath worn on his calf and held it by the blade. The monkey stepped forward, shockingly human-like in its movements, and swung at him with its left hand curled in a semi-fist. Bones ducked the punch and answered with an uppercut right hand holding the knife butt first. He slammed the steel butt into the monkey's chin, sending the new world primate into the air briefly before it landed on its back. Bones was prepared to attack again, Willis and Maddock backing him up, but the dazed animal lay there, eyeing them but not making a move.

"Stay down if you know what's good for you!" Bones wagged a finger at the defeated beast. Maddock was already eyeballing their forward track, searching for cameras, movement, anything, while Willis pondered the monkey.

"It ain't normal for monkeys to be so aggressive. I've

been around a bunch, in Africa, southeast Asia...sure they can fight, like any animal if you mess with it, but we've been jumped by two different kinds of monkeys since we've been in Haiti, and everybody keeps saying there used to be monkeys here but not anymore. What gives?"

Maddock looked away from the trees and ground up ahead, satisfied they were not being observed. He considered the primate, which now rolled to one side and scampered off into the underbrush while Bones flipped it a silent bird. "What worries me is that monkey betrayed no emotion while it attacked."

Bones nodded, making eye contact with Maddock. "Like those freaking zombie people" Bones said. "You don't think..."

Rustling noise ensued from the plants behind them, the way they had come. Maddock spun around and took in the source of the ruckus.

"More monkeys! Run!"

Chapter 35

Avila's Island

Fabi had no intentions of waiting around to see what Avila had in store for her. Although she had no access to tools of any kind, her pockets having been searched and everything taken by Avila's guards, she worked at her bonds by wriggling her slender wrists back and forth. A stifled cry of pain escaped her lips as she wrenched her joints in ways they were never designed. But at last her hands came sliding free of the restraints.

She heard footsteps approaching from outside the room, hard-soled shoes on stone and stuck her freed hands behind her back as if she was still bound. She tried to sit still and calm her breathing so as not to show signs of her recent exertion.

A lab worker she did not recognize entered holding a leather case of some kind. He made brief eye contact with her from behind clear plastic safety goggles, then walked behind Fabi toward a counter. She heard him unzip the case, followed by the clatter of unknown instruments on the counter. He spoke soon after that.

"I'm going to administer you something that should make you feel more comfortable, more relaxed and open to discussion. It won't hurt a bit."

Fabi heard the man step back toward her chair. She prayed he wouldn't notice her unbound hand but a second later he was leaning over in front of her, eyeing a bare spot on her right arm.

"What do you think you're doing? What is that? I don't want it!"

He held up an alcohol swab in one hand, lowering the syringe a bit in the other. "Now, now. Just relax. Here you go." The lab tech bent down to administer the shot and sprang into motion. The tech reared up as the arm he was about to shoot moved, but he was far too late.

She grabbed him by his curly mop of hair, yanked his head down, and drove her knee up to meet him. He slumped to the ground, stunned by the blow. He began to groan, and she kicked him in the temple, hard, but not hard enough to be lethal, and he fell silent.

"I guess they forgot to tell you some girls know how to fight."

Fabi stripped him of his lab coat and donned it. She figured it might distract some people for a few seconds, at least, and sometimes that was all she needed. She looked around the room briefly to see if there was anything she could use as a weapon, but saw nothing and hurried on. She had to find Cassandra. Where was she now?

Fabi slipped into the next room, where half a dozen people lay strapped to beds, each receiving intravenous treatment of some sort. A couple of them looked at her with glassy eyes but the rest were sleeping or heavily medicated. Another thought she didn't have time for flashed through her mind—what was Dr. Avila doing here with these people? They didn't appear to be regular patients. Many of the more common machines were missing altogether, although there was no shortage of equipment in general; it was just that most of it was unidentifiable to Fabi.

She hurried through this eerie space to a closed door at the end of the room. She reached out to open it and then felt someone grab her from behind. Instinctively, she snapped her head back, cracking her unseen assailant across the bridge of the nose. She heard a cry of pain and shook the man off. Whirling around to finish the job, Fabi was instantly deflated to find herself facing, in addition to her attacker, an armed guard with a pistol aimed at her chest...and Avila himself.

The physician's expression was stern as he stared down Fabi while her bloody-faced attacker backed away from her with a hateful glare. Avila wagged his head side to side while making clucking noises.

"Fabiola...I am growing impatient by the minute. If you continue to refuse cooperation, you leave me no choice but to take more rigorous measures, measures that you will not find palatable in the least, I can assure you." Having slunk back to the corner, the guard who had attacked Fabi licked his lips.

Fabi ignored him and focused on Avila. "I've been extensively trained to resist torture, Dr. Avila." She put on a brave front but her insides threatened to turn to water at the thought.

Avila smiled and turned to his armed guard. "Enough nonsense. Take that lab coat off her and then bring her back to her bed. I think it's time we used the formula."

Chapter 36

Maddock, Bones and Willis dashed through the jungle, chased by the shrieks and howls of the troop of primates in hot pursuit. Willis looked over at Maddock and patted the pistol he wore in a shoulder holster. "Why don't we just pop a cap in a couple of these things? The rest of them will get the message and leave."

Maddock jumped over a tree root and kept going. "We don't want to let Avila's men know we're here." He slowed to duck beneath a low-hanging branch. "And armed."

Looking back, Maddock could see the monkeys were easily gaining on them. A confrontation was inevitable. The SEAL-turned-treasure hunter drew his dive knife. "We'll have to do this old-school. Stand your ground."

Maddock stopped with his back to the trunk of a large tree and faced the oncoming assemblage of primates. Willis and Bones also unsheathed their blades and prepared to fight. The prospect of facing down about a dozen animals roughly the same size as they were, but with body mass consisting mostly of pure muscle, was a daunting one.

Maddock hoped the humans' intelligence and use of tools—the knives—would be sufficient advantage. He knew they could go to their pistols as a last resort, but giving their position away would compromise the extraction mission. He reminded himself as he always had on these types of missions that a person waited somewhere close by, probably in dire circumstances, counting on him to get them out.

Then the monkeys reached them, and a full-scale melee erupted in the jungle. Sharp nails scored Maddock's flesh. Strong hands sought to gouge his eyes. Dark fur and white teeth flashed before him as he fought. Mad, bestial shrieks drowned out all other sound, save for a few choice curses from Bones. *This is crazy*, Maddock thought as he slashed with his blade and another attacker fell.

It was grisly work, but the blades made all the difference. The crazed monkeys kept coming, drone-like in their single-mindedness, until the last lay on the ground.

Maddock and the others had suffered a few cuts and large bruises, but thankfully no bites. He didn't know if whatever had turned the primates into automatons could be transferred, and he didn't want to find out. Willis removed his boot from beneath the carcass of a dead monkey and shook his head slowly. "I hate that we were forced to do this."

Maddock nodded in agreement. "Avila did this. I'm sure of it."

"Me too." Bones holstered his knife. "In that email Fabi sent, she mentioned something about Avila's weird experiments in that clinic."

Willis looked up from the pile of monkeys. "All that only makes me want to get at this Dr. Avila guy even more."

"So let's do it." Bones walked toward the edge of the small clearing in which they had battled the monkeys. With a last glance at the fallen primates, Maddock and Willis followed him deeper into the island forest.

The foliage grew thicker as they penetrated further into the island's interior, and it grew increasingly difficult to move steadily and silently. All the while they were looking over their shoulders for new threats. Finally, light appeared up ahead and they saw a clearing. Maddock and Willis crouched behind a stand of banana palms and they discovered they now faced a different threat; an even deadlier one.

A head-high rock wall surrounded Dr. Avila's compound, which Maddock knew from Letson's satellite photos to consist of a main mansion and several outbuildings. What occupied his attention now, though, was the open gate set into the rock wall, with a guard standing in front of it.

He was armed with an automatic rifle and smoked a cigarette. Maddock was glad to recognize his demeanor for the detachment and boredom it represented; this guy was probably near the end of his shift, a long day on his feet where nothing happened for hours at a time. Such was the situation for guards the world over—the difficulty was in maintaining a state of readiness for what could require split-second reactions in the face of ongoing tedium.

Willis shot Maddock a look that said, *now*? Maddock mouthed the word, *wait*, and Willis nodded, returning his gaze to the smoking guard.

As they watched, a long-haired figure materialized out of the trees and pistol-whipped the guard on the back of the head, dropping him instantly. Bones dragged his body out of sight behind an SUV parked nearby and then joined his comrades at their hiding spot.

"Told you I could do it."

Maddock and Willis looked at one another and shook their heads.

Bones threw his hands up. "What?"

Maddock waved a hand dismissively. "Don't worry about it. Let's just hope you haven't rattled that guy's brain too badly. We need him to tell us how to get inside."

Chapter 37

Fabi lay strapped to a cot in the same room she had found so eerie, the one with a group of people she had initially thought of as patients. Now, as she struggled to move her hands and feet against the shackles that chained her to the bed, she understood they were in fact more like subjects. Humans being experimented on by Dr. Avila...for what purpose she didn't know.

The squeak of cot wheels drew near and then the door pushed open as a lab tech and a security guard wheeled in a new cot. Fabi lifted her head as high as she could, straining her neck muscles.

"Cassandra!" She couldn't stop herself from blurting out her friend's name. But apparently Cassandra had been sedated already, because she was slow to respond. Her eyelids appeared heavy as she turned to look in Fabi's general direction, as if searching for the source of the voice.

Another man strode into the room, gaze shifting from Fabi to the tech and the guard, from there to Cassandra and back to Fabi. Dr. Avila spoke to Fabi while observing his employees wheel the cot to a station with a cluster of waiting IVs and machines. "She's already been prepped for the main event, shall we say. She's a bit unresponsive at the moment, so you'll likely find her to be a less than exciting conversationalist right about now."

"Don't give her any more drugs, Dr. Avila. Please. She did not consent to this. You're a *physician*, for crying out loud. What about the Hippocratic oath you took, the one that said you would always strive to keep your patients' best interests at heart?"

Avila glanced over at Cassandra, who was now having her arm wiped with an alcohol pad by the lab tech, then quickly back to Fabi. "She's not a patient. She's a subject. Unless perhaps..."

"Perhaps what?" Fabi watched as the lab tech now uncapped a needle and held it poised over Cassandra's chained arm.

"Perhaps you could tell me what I want to know about the treasure, and then I will withdraw this..." He nodded in Cassandra's direction. "...*subject* from the experiment."

Fabi slammed her head back against the thin cot, rattling its flimsy frame. "I told you already, Dr. Avila, I don't know anything about any treasure. Okay, maybe my cousin David was looking for one; he had mentioned that to me a few times, but I wasn't privy to the details."

Avila gave a long exhalation before nodding to his lab tech, who promptly jabbed the needle into Cassandra's flesh and depressed the plunger. He raised his voice over Fabi's protests. "Listen to me: it takes one hour for the effects to take hold. Until they do, the treatment is reversible. Beyond that time..."

He looked over at Cassandra, her head lolling back and forth on the sweat-stained cot. He made an exaggerated and wholly insincere expression of sadness.

Fabi yelled at the top of her lungs. "I don't know where it is!"

Avila shrugged. "I guess in an hour I'll believe you." He turned away from Fabi and huddled with his lab tech in quiet conference in a corner of the room while the armed guard stood watch. Unable to do anything else, Fabi called out to Cassandra.

"Cassandra! Can you hear me? It's okay, hang in there, you'll be okay."

Cassandra uttered a couple of nonsensical words but never focused her eyes on Fabi while she tossed her head back and forth. She seemed to drift in and out of consciousness. Avila and his tech ignored them while the guard looked on passively, apparently concerned only with action, not words. Fabi continued attempting to communicate with her friend over the next few minutes, but her condition only deteriorated, taking her even farther from reality.

"Dr. Avila! *Why* are you doing this?"

The physician held a finger up to his lab tech and slowly turned around to face Fabi. "Why? To make people better, of course." He beamed as though he had just uttered the most fantastic thing a person could ever say.

"How does carrying out unregulated experimentation on non-consenting subjects make people better?"

Avila took a deep breath, as though gathering his patience. "Fabiola, you are still a relatively young person, somewhat naive. How can I put this?" He stared at Cassandra while wrinkling his eyebrows into a mask of contemplation before continuing.

"Many people are nothing more than simple drudges. Near-mindless automatons, going about their daily life chores with a robotic detachment best suited to...well, suited to machine-like labor, really. That's where my HAITI project comes in. It stands for Human-Animal Initiative for Total Indoctrination."

Fabi bristled with hate as she recalled seeing the name of the project in the clinic files, blissfully unaware at the time of its abhorrent meaning.

Avila went on. "Why not let the zombie class serve the more capable, yes—dare I say it—*better*, more advanced people, people who will afford them a life of productivity, free from criminal urges?"

"A person's station in life should not be dictated to them by someone else, Dr. Avila, that's why not. You're not talking about naturally letting people land where they may, are you? Why else would you need to drug them?" She nodded to Cassandra, who had stopped the constant thrashing but now uttered a continuous, low moan.

"I am simply accelerating their natural fate and harnessing it where it can do the most good." He also nodded to Cassandra. "Don't pretend you haven't noticed that her skills are not exactly irreplaceable. I suspect that on your first day, you've already demonstrated you can outperform her."

"What about free will?"

Avila laughed. "Free will is wasted on the inferior. Look at how the lowest of the low exercise it: murder, rape, theft, and countless other crimes."

"That's a messed up version of law enforcement."

"There are more applications, though. Drug addiction would be thing of the past. Population could be strictly controlled. So many possibilities, and what is the real cost? Insignificant sacrifice by inconsequential people."

"It's the worst kind of slavery," Fabi said. "But something else is going on."

Out of the corner of her eye, Fabi caught the lab tech glance up sharply from his cart of instruments, waiting for Avila's reaction, which was a hollow laugh.

"Let's just say there are certain applications for this work that others will pay handsomely for."

"Like what?" A cold fear, like ice water coursing through her veins, gripped Fabi.

"You served in the military. Imagine a fighting force that never disobeyed an order and never quailed in the face of the enemy. Fearsome, to be sure."

"You're crazy, Dr. Avila, you know that? You can't possibly understand the full ramifications of this....this zombification process you're playing with. What if it gets out of hand and you can't control the people you change?" She eyed Cassandra with dismay.

Avila glanced over at his tech, who promptly lowered his gaze and went back to shuffling his instruments around on the cart. Avila looked back to Fabi and said, "We're working on a 'switch' so that we'll be able to turn the abilities on and off. We're almost there, isn't that right, Peter?"

The tech looked up and gave a nod that lacked true enthusiasm. "We're working on it."

"That's why you want the treasure, isn't it?" Fabi spat. "To fund your sick experiments."

"That is part of it, you're right. But the other part is that the 1715 Spanish treasure is in fact rightfully mine. I have an ancestor, a distant relative, who was the ship's doctor on that ill-fated voyage. Cristobal D'Avila was his name. I still share his same pure, Spanish blood. Our family has never permitted our noble bloodline to be diluted by intermarrying with commoners."

Avila could see Fabi's eyes widening, and he leaned toward her to emphasize his last point. "When my work here is completed, I believe it will pave the way for me to rule in Haiti, as it should be."

Fabi eyed him with unadulterated disgust. "Consider this my resignation, Dr. Avila. I can't believe I spent so much time working for such a monster."

Sudden, spastic convulsions racked Cassandra's body. She let out a guttural, pain-addled scream. When she settled back down, Avila said, "You will share her fate, you know, if you can't tell me where this treasure is. This is your last chance." He nodded to his tech and the man wheeled his cart full of instruments over to Fabi, still strapped down in the cot. The tech adjusted an IV stand and swabbed her arm, preparing to insert a needle. Cassandra caterwauled again and Fabi looked over at her.

"Okay! Hold it! I'll talk."

Chapter 38

Maddock, Bones and Willis slipped unseen past the guarded front entrance to Avila's main house. After coercing information from the front gate guard by scaring but not actually hurting him, they had left the man trussed up outside the gate and made their way here.

"Back door should be on this side." Maddock crouched low and pointed to the house. Bones and Willis nodded. They were about to move out when something stirred in the waist-high brush that surrounded much of the house. A man rose about twenty-five feet in front of them and walked toward them without speaking. The person had a slackjawed look about him, lifeless eyes and a deathly pallor about the skin.

"More over here!" Bones pointed to the right.

"And here!" Willis indicated their left flank.

Maddock pointed at a forty-five degree angle to their left, toward the back door the guard had told them about. More *zombii* poured out of the brush and stalked after the three intruders. The treasure seekers ran for the back door, slipping through gaps in the zombie ranks before sprinting the rest of the way to the house.

A chain link fence surrounded the house close to the door, with a gate that was closed and locked. Worse, a guard patrolled the area between the house and the gate, pacing the narrow space up and back. Maddock tapped Bones on the arm.

"You take care of the gate. Willis, you're on zombie duty. I'll handle the guard."

Willis held up a hand. "Hold up, there's gotta be at least a dozen of those things coming this way. I can't take 'em all out, at least not without making some noise." He patted his holstered pistol.

Maddock tilted his head toward Bones, who was already

moving to the gate. "You know how Bones is with locks. Shouldn't be very long. But if that guard sees us and raises the alarm..." He turned and looked back to the approaching zombie squad. "My guess is that we could end up as one of those things."

Willis nodded. He turned around and headed a little ways back through the brush while Maddock crept off to the left, a rock in one hand. When Maddock saw the guard turn around and begin walking back in their direction, he tossed the rock along the fence. When it landed the guard spun around and moved his weapon to the ready position before moving off to investigate.

Maddock breathed a sigh of relief and looked back to check on Bones, who had thankfully just sprung the lock. Maddock then looked around for Willis and saw two shadowy figures circling in a fighting dance. He went to Willis and dispatched the combatant zombie by pistol whipping it in the skull. It crumpled to the ground, but three more were heading their way.

"Come, let's get inside." Maddock and Willis turned and ran to Bones at the gate. The *zombii* closed fast and the men hurried inside the fence without closing the gate, running for the door. As they reached it, the guard walked around the corner of a metal utility housing, where Willis grabbed him, pinning his arms to his sides, while Bones relieved him of his weapon and Maddock took the swipe card he wore on a lanyard around his neck.

The sound of approaching zombie footsteps neared, and they moved on to the door on this side of the house. When they got to it, Bones tried it and found it locked. He pointed to the card reader. Maddock took a glance back at the *zombii* before pulling the card through. A light turned green and Bones pulled the door open. He stood there a moment, straining to see what was inside, but Willis shoved him in. ""'Go! Go! They're coming!"

Bones and Willis entered the building first. Maddock followed, pulling the door shut just as they heard the guard scream as the *zombii* got to him and began to maul.

Chapter 39

A wave of bitter self-loathing coursed through Fabi as she unburdened herself to her captor. She hated herself for what she was doing. She'd been trained to resist interrogation, but now she was broken. Damn! She'd believed herself tougher than this. Apparently, she wasn't.

"And so Maddock, Bones and Willis went diving off Alto Velo Island to look for the wreck, and I haven't heard from them since." Fabi looked up from the cot at Avila, tears streaming down her face, sobbing and gasping for breath. "That's everything."

It had been an emotional recounting of events. The facts, stories and memories poured out of her. Once she began telling the truth, she held nothing back, as if a floodgates had opened and she could do nothing to close them. Avila looked down on her with a wide smile.

"Shhh, there now, Fabi. You've done well! Calm down, now. Take it easy..." Fabi closed her eyes for a moment, to block out the reality of this weird place, to try to calm down a bit...but when she opened them again Avila was wearing a respirator mask and placing an inhaler like the kind used by those with asthma into her mouth. With her wrists cuffed to the cot rails, she couldn't fend him off, and he squeezed two puffs of whatever the inhaler contained into her mouth before she could move her head away from it.

"There you are. That should calm you down." Avila retreated from the cot and handed his lab technician the inhaler and his mask, both of which the tech handled with gloved hands and the abundance of caution reserved for material that represented a biohazard.

Perhaps it was the contents of the inhaler, perhaps not, but Fabi did, in fact, feel calmer. Self-loathing burned through the fear, and left only anger. She looked Avila in the eyes and somehow knew that he would not let her go. She had to find a way. Perhaps if she could get him to lower his guard.

"I don't understand how you even made this zombie formula, or whatever it is."

Avila grinned. "The ancestor I mentioned, Cristobal, had an encounter with *zombii*. From an early age I was fascinated with the story, and researching the phenomenon became one of mypassions." He settled into a chair, a faraway look in his eyes.

He's letting his guard down, Fabi thought. *If I could only get loose.* "What did you find?" she asked, trying to keep him distracted.

"I knew the scientist in you would come out eventually. I discovered that most of the reports were garbage: religious frenzy, mental illness, mind-altering drugs, brain damage, even a few cases of someone being buried alive. But in some rare cases I discovered people whose brain functioning had actually changed. The centers that control inhibitions and original thought were "turned off" for lack of a better term. I knew that this phenomenon existed in nature, with certain ants, for example, so I investigated it from a biological perspective. Those who knew the true secrets were reluctant to divulge them, but I...persuaded them. I discovered certain plants that, when used in combination, elicited this effect."

"What's to stop others from simply duplicating your work?"

"Fair question. We constantly work to collect all the plant material on the island and then used herbicide to eradicate anything we might miss. It is my intention to control the entire supply of the needed material."

Fabi was running out of questions and was no closer to freeing herself. "So, you grow it here?"

"Grow, synthesize, experiment. In fact, you're helping with one of our experiments right now."

Fabi's heart raced. The aerosol! "What do you mean? What did you give me?"

Avila's grin did little to assuage Fabi's concern, his

words even less so. "We're experimenting with transferring the productivity therapy via aerosol, and it so happens that you're the first test case."

Chapter 40

Maddock, Bones, and Willis jumped when the lights came on in the back entranceway to the house.

"Chill, it's just motion-activated." Willis lay a hand on Bones' gun arm.

"I hear footsteps. Down there." Maddock pointed to the end of the short hallway in which they found themselves. The trio of operators slipped silently to the end of the hall, Bones and Willis to the right and left, respectively, while Maddock crouched in the middle. Footsteps grew louder from the left. Willis tensed, his pistol in the ready position.

"Clear," Bones subvocalized, letting Willis and Maddock know there were no immediate threats coming from their right side. When the guard reached the hallway, Willis reached up and pulled him in, wrestling him to the ground. What he didn't count on was the immediate gunfire from the left side, down the hall. Someone was backing up his fellow guard.

Maddock returned fire down the hall while Willis and Bones incapacitated the other guard, binding his wrists and ankles with plastic zip-ties and relieving him of his weapon, a snub-nosed semi-automatic. When the guard was under control, Willis assumed a prone sniper position and belly-crawled to the edge of the hallway where he joined Maddock in laying down fire to the left. That guard retreated and Maddock and the others pushed forward into the hallway, to the right. They reached an open door on the left side and entered a holding cell area where *zombii* in different states were held. Some were more human than others, with the ability to speak, though others were mostly animals at this point with little or no capacity for independent thought. And some were in fact actual animals that Maddock recognized from their monkey encounters.

"Creepy as all get-out." Willis eyed a monstrous ape-like form that resembled one of the largest primates they had defeated. Bones and Maddock agreed with Willis, with Maddock vowing to put an end to this experimentation when and if they got out of here with Fabi alive.

They continued on into another room that functioned as a ward of sorts, with people strapped down in cots, connected to IV drips and electronic monitor machines. They moved through this space as well, lamenting there was no time to help these individuals right now, but knowing that bringing down Avila himself would be the best thing they could do for everyone involved.

Bones tried the closed door at the opposite end of the room and found it locked, but Maddock swiped his appropriated key card and it opened. They entered yet another lab, each wondering what lengths Dr. Avila had gone to in order to develop his hideous creations. This room featured isles of lab benches stacked high with traditional chemistry equipment—ring stands, beakers, Erlenmeyer flasks, racks of test tubes—and they almost didn't see the guard hunched over one of the benches.

He was reading a magazine, oblivious to the room's new occupants. Willis popped up behind him and clocked him hard, but not too hard, on the neck where it joined the base of the skull. The man slumped off his bench, unconscious, and was caught by Willis before his head could crack on the concrete floor. Willis eased the man into a prostrate position and again, they relieved him of his weapons and swipe card.

Maddock was less than entirely pleased with the outcome. "Guys, we need to be able to question at least one of these guys so we can find out where Fabi is being held. Can't knock them all out cold right away every time."

Willis gave a sheepish look. "Sorry. Instinct, you know."

The lab now clear of resistance with no incoming threats detected, the three of them took some time to walk around and see what they could learn. Bones moved to one area that contained grow lights hanging from the ceiling over a soil bed of various plants. He moved among them, examining them closely. He rubbed the leaves of one between his fingertips and sniffed it. "Hey, I know this one. Sassafras, My grandmother swore by this stuff."

"Swore by it for what?" Willis wanted to know.

"Anti-inflammatory and insect bite treatment. It's been banned in the U.S. Doesn't surprise me that…"

A scream rent the air from somewhere outside the lab. A female scream. Bones turned and headed for the far exit, Maddock and Willis following a split second later.

"Fabi!"

Chapter 41

Maddock burst into the room at the same time as Bones, with Willis a step behind them. Fabi lay strapped to a cot while Avila stood over her with a syringe pressed to her neck.

"Stop where you are! Do not make another move or she gets it!"

Maddock froze, holding Bones and Willis back, lest emotions get the better of them, especially Bones. "Gets what?"

"This syringe contains a high concentration of potassium chloride, more than enough to stop her heart. If one of you so much as flinches, she gets the needle."

No one spoke for a few seconds, but Avila could see the three warriors visually appraising the situation. Bones focused on Fabi while Willis inspected the room, his gaze lingering on Cassanda, who was no longer moving as she lay strapped to a cot not far from Fabi. Maddock's eyes were fixed on the doctor himself. The cool scrutiny apparently made Avila nervous enough to want to reiterate his position.

"You might be able to kill me, but I assure you she will die. If you don't want that to happen, drop your weapons and slide them over to me."

Maddock noted that Avila crouched behind the cot—and Fabi—in such a way as to block his chest and even part of his head. It was an effective stance, for now, but at least he was scared. Apparently he'd been caught without his guard duty. Three on one, with the hostage Avila's only saving grace. As dire as the situation was, Maddock had faced worse. He knew their best chance—Fabi's best chance, that was—was to play along until Avila slipped up. Being a non-professional in the combat business, he surely would. Still, the weapons loss was an undeniable blow. Maddock and the others reluctantly slid their pistols and dive knives across to Avila, where they came to rest beneath Fabi's cot. Avila's right foot swept beneath the cot to draw the pile of weaponry closer to him.

"I want the three of you to lie face down on the floor right now." Avila jerked the hand holding the needle to Fabi's neck as a warning.

"Dr. Avila, please think about what you're doing," Maddock tried to reason. "There's no way out for you once you go down this road. You'll be just another common criminal."

Fabi's sudden outburst jarred them all. "Let him kill me! Don't do what he says! He'll kill all of us, or even worse, turn us into zombies."

Maddock heard her words, but he also heard the terror in her voice. She did not want to die. She did not want to be zombified, either. And looking at Cassandra, Maddock could see that whatever she had been injected with had done her no good. She was out cold, face covered in foamy froth. Was this the fate Avila had intended for Fabi had Maddock not intervened?

"You've got five seconds to comply!" Avila gripped Fabi's shoulder harder as he kept the needle pressed up to her neck.

Seeing no choice at the moment other than to comply with Avila's demands, Maddock eased himself face down to the floor, arms and legs outstretched. Bones and Willis followed suit. Just because he was lying down didn't mean Maddock had given up, though. He continued trying to appeal to whatever sense of humanity Avila might still possess.

"Your creations are running amok all over your lab, Dr. Avila. Your men are down. Why don't you put an end to this before more people, including yourself, get hurt?"

Avila laughed heartily without loosening his death grip on Fabi. "Have you not heard the old expression? If at first you don't succeed..."

"Die, die again?" Willis grunted.

Avila glared at him and looked back to Maddock. "I'll

just have to start over, if not here, then somewhere else. There is no doubt that my discoveries will make me the most powerful man in the world."

Bones strained his neck to look up from the floor in order to glare at Avila. "You're a sick freak, you know that?"

The physician grinned in return. "Perhaps someday you will see the wisdom in my actions. If you can bite your tongue long enough to live through this, that is."

During the exchange, Maddock eyed the most interesting thing he could see from his worm's eye vantage point: the pile of weapons on the floor underneath the cot. He knew that Avila had been reticent to lean down and try to pick one of them up while the three of them were standing. But now that they were prostrate on the floor, he was bound to make a move for them. And then it would be all but over. Bones kept the distracting dialogue going while Maddock's tactical wheels turned.

"What's up with you, Avila? You're not a short guy, so it must not be a Napoleon complex that you have. I guess you're compensating for shortcomings in other physical areas, is that it?"

Avila cackled in Bones' direction. "Personal insults are tools of the feeble-minded."

Maddock sensed the time was near to make a move. He only hoped his friends would somehow know what he was thinking. He looked over at Bones and caught the twinkle in his eye.

"Why don't you just fight me, Avila? I'll even do it blindfolded." It was not lost on Maddock that Bones sounded truly angry, no doubt incensed by the fact that his woman, or one of them, anyway, was in peril at the whim of this madman.

Maddock watched as Avila again turned his attention to Bones. While he delivered an angry retort, something about his time having been wasted long enough by a descendent of savages, Maddock reached back and slipped a recon knife from the inside of his boot. He'd taken to carrying them that way in his Navy days, and he still made a habit of it. He palmed the blade under his hand and wrist as he continued to lie face down, surreptitiously watching Avila.

"Charming as it was, I'm afraid our conversation must come to an end." Avila leaned down and made a grab for the abandoned weapons, and Maddock sprang into action, rising to his feet. He hurled his knife at Avila, who turned his head. The blade sliced him across the cheek, leaving a red stripe, and clattered to the floor somewhere behind him.

Avila raised one of the pistols he'd snatched from the floor but Maddock was already in motion, rapidly chewing up the distance between him and the menacing doctor. He only hoped he would be quick enough.

Maddock leapt as the explosion of a gunshot filled his ears.

Chapter 42

Avila's bullet buzzed past Maddock, but he felt the projectile clip his shoulder. It wasn't enough to stop his forward momentum, though, and he crashed into Avila over the cot. Fabi squealed while Avila bear-hugged Maddock and pulled him to the floor on his side of the cot.

Maddock gripped Avila's gun hand as the physician fought against his opponent's grip to bring his weapon to bear. Maddock unleashed a flurry of jabs to Avila's face with his left hand, but Avila was still managing to level the pistol at Maddock's head. He fired once as Maddock dodged to the left, feeling his hair move as the round passed through it into the ceiling, exploding a light fixture that rained glass down upon them.

Maddock caught motion out of his peripheral vision but couldn't stop grappling with Avila long enough to see what it was. Then suddenly Bones popped up behind and to the right of Avila, his own firearm jammed up against the doctor's temple.

"It's time to die, Dr. Moreau."

Avila's eyes widened in fear as he froze. Maddock extricated himself from Avila, relieving him of his handgun in the process. Once at arm's length from his foe, Maddock rose to his feet, dusting off his pants.

"Bones, I had no idea you had any literary inclinations whatsoever. In the service the only thing I ever saw you reading was *Playboy*, and something tells me it wasn't for the articles."

Bones shrugged without taking the barrel off of Avila. "I have read a couple of books, you know. Now and then."

"Will you two shut up!" Avila barked.

"Don't worry, mad scientist, you won't have to listen to us for much longer." Bones centered his barrel on Avila's temple.

"Have some sense!" Avila pleaded. "Spare my life in the name of humanity! Scientific advancement!"

Maddock waved an arm at the destroyed lab, a dead zombie body crumpled on the floor in a corner, Cassandra's limp body in the cot next to Fabi's. "This is what you call advancement? Experimenting with people without their consent in order to turn them into some kind of slaves?"

"Not slaves. Productive workers. To better their own lives as well as those they work for."

"What a crock," Bones growled. "You know, the Nazis experimented with Jewish prisoners during the war and they were later held accountable for their actions."

"I'm well aware of the Nuremberg Trials." Avila's voice had lowered to a near whisper.

Bones nodded. "Well, consider this your trial. And we've found you guilty. Goodbye, Dr. Scumbag."

"Don't do it, Bones!" Fabi's shrill plea rent the air.

Bones narrowed his eyes without averting his gaze from Avila's head. "Give me one good reason why not."

"If you kill him, you'll have to kill me too."

Chapter 43

"What do you mean, Fabi?" Maddock gave Bones a look that said *hold off.* He kept the gun pressed up against Avila's head, but refrained from pulling the trigger.

"He injected me with something. He's going to make me into one of those…things. He has to reverse it. I'd rather you kill me first, Bones, than me turn into...into..." She couldn't complete her morbid thought, and Avila cut in.

"Not going to happen."

Bones' eyes oozed hatred as he stared at him. "When I was in the SEALs, Avila, they taught me a few tricks about how to persuade people. It's been a little while since I had to do something like that, but even so, I doubt you want to be the one I use to brush up on my skills."

He reached down and grabbed Avila by the base of the neck with the hand not holding the gun, confident that Maddock or Willis would take him down if he somehow did manage to wrest Bones' gun from him. But Avila's reaction was simply to laugh.

"Don't waste your time. There is no cure. I lied to her to get her to tell me where the treasure is."

"That's a load of horse manure if I ever smelled it." Bones looked to Maddock, expecting him to concur, but Maddock's expression bore a trace of uncertainty. He tried to hide it but inside, his heart sank. Something about Avila told him he was telling the truth. Maddock was formulating his next thought when they heard a commotion from a short distance away.

A man Maddock didn't recognize, wearing a white lab coat, burst into the room. He was quickly followed by a couple of armed men. Avila's eyes bugged out at the sight of his associates. He called out to his men.

"The big one has a gun on me! All three are armed!" Seeing that Bones' gaze was averted to the newcomers, Avila launched his body hard against Bones' legs, knocking him backward and throwing off his aim.

The newly arrived gunmen opened fire with semi-automatic weapons, sending Maddock and Willis diving for cover while returning bursts of rounds loosed from the hip. Computer screens exploded, puffs of drywall dust filled the air and a broken pipe sprayed hot water.

Maddock took position beneath a lab bench and loaded a fresh clip into his weapon. He then proceeded to unleash a more carefully aimed salvo at Avila's men. Willis did the same from his own cover position a few feet away. To Maddock, it felt like old times, though not in a good way. He'd never liked killing, but it was something he would do if he had to, especially as a SEAL. Yet it saddened him that he'd come here as a peaceful treasure hunter only to be confronted with a kind of savagery worse than that usually encountered in war.

Out of the corner of his eye, Maddock saw a young woman—the same one who'd been been strapped down minutes before—leap onto Avila's back. Before the surprised doctor could fight back, she sank her teeth into his throat. Avila's shriek died in a wet gurgle, and was drowned out as one of his men gunned down the crazed attacker.

The firefight lasted only a few more moments. Once Avila's gunmen were down, Maddock glanced back over to Bones to see how he was doing. The big Cherokee was leaning down over Avila, taking his pulse. He looked up at Maddock and shook his head. "He's dead, and good riddance."

Fabi who was now free of her bonds, hurried over and knelt beside the girl. "Cass," she whispered. Tears streamed down her face. "I'm so sorry." She looked up at Bones. "I let her go. I just couldn't stand to see her lying here. I guess I thought she might still be herself, but that stuff…"

"It's all right." Bones offered his hand and helped her up.

She stood and squeezed Bones in a tight embrace. "Thank you for saving me." She turned to look at Maddock and Willis. I want to tell all of you… I love you guys. I just wanted to say it before...before I turn into one of those things. Avila was my last chance."

"Maybe not." Maddock strode across the lab floor toward the lone man of the three interlopers who was still standing, the unarmed man in the lab coat. He stood there, shell-shocked, as Maddock grabbed him by the collar.

"What's your name?"

"P-Peter!"

"Peter, what is the cure for this condition that Dr. Avila gave to her?" He pointed to Fabi.

The man shook his head, a sad look spreading across his face. "There is none. I'm very sorry. If there was I would gladly administer it to her, but there isn't."

Maddock shook him. "What is your role here? Are you a scientist or a technician or what?"

"I am but one of the scientists who developed the serum according to Dr. Avila's specifications." He nodded to Avila's dead body before continuing. "We were working on a 'switch'—a biochemical trigger that would allow the zombification process to be turned on and off at will—but to date that line of development has not been successful."

"How does the actual serum, without the switch, work?" Maddock demanded.

"You can think of it sort of like a fast-acting cancer that doesn't usually go to completion, that is, clinical death. It modifies the blood cells at first, and from there it metastasizes to the brain. It takes about an hour for the serum to take effect, and once it does the change is progressive and permanent." He glanced over at Fabi as if expecting her to transform into a mindless monster at any second.

Maddock followed his gaze. "Fabi, how long ago did Avila inject you with the serum?"

She looked at him over Bones' shoulder, sniffling. "About forty-five minutes."

Maddock looked back to Peter, still held in his iron grip. "We have to try something. Let's inject her with the latest batch of the switch serum that you do have and hope it works."

But the scientist's eyes were more downcast than ever. "We used the last batch we had on some monkeys. I'm terribly sorry, but it takes at least forty-eight hours to cook up each batch. We didn't keep it in production mode, it was just sort of a side project that—"

The sound of Bones' footsteps slamming the floor caused him to break off while both he and Maddock watched his friend run to the far side of the lab. Maddock released his hold on the scientist, who staggered back a couple of steps, composing himself while he looked around the shambles of his former laboratory in disgust.

"Bones, where are you going?" As Maddock watched, his former partner in war, now partner in business, stopped at a shattered plant growing station. He moved about there for a few minutes, not responding to Maddock, Willis and Fabi asking him if he was all right. Then he came running back across the lab, clutching a syringe full of dark liquid.

He went to Fabi, and before she could say, "What is that?" he injected her with the substance.

"Fingers crossed," he said.

Then Peter said, "We really need to get out of here. None of us are safe, trust me."

"Which way?" Maddock looked past him to the nearest lab exit.

"I can lead us out through the house."

Maddock held his gaze while he hefted his pistol. "If this is some kind of double-cross..."

The researcher shook his head. "Just trying to avoid any more killing and get out of here with what little dignity I have left. Helping you will let me redeem myself, at least a bit."

Maddock's internal guide told him that the man was being forthcoming. "Lead the way. Wills, Bones, Fabi—let's move." They began moving out as a group, but Fabi looked back at Cassandra." We can't leave her."

"Fabi, she's gone. If we try to carry her body out, it'll

slow us down. It's not worth the risk."

Fabi broke down in a fresh bout of tears while Peter pleaded with his eyes for Bones to get her moving.

"We can't just leave her here like this!"

Bones gently urged her along. "We'll send the authorities back for her body after we get out of here safely."

They set out again but this time it was Maddock who halted after a short distance.

"Now what's up?" Bones asked.

"Hold on, one minute." Maddock moved to the bank of cages on the far wall and released the dozens of *zombii* corralled inside before running back to the group.

"Let them cover our trail."

Chapter 44

"We may encounter some resistance when we go through here," Peter warned.

"Resistance is my specialty." Bones held his firearm in the ready position, and Willis followed suit. Maddock asked the scientist what sort of resistance they could expect.

"Living and not-so-living, but it's Avila's guards who haven't yet gotten the memo that worry me the most. There may not be time to explain things to them, and they're more of a shoot-first-and-ask-questions-later bunch. I'll try to let them know, but first let's get you guys out of here so they won't be so nervous."

They emerged from the lab complex into the actual mansion, leaving the door wide open. Distant shouting echoed, but other than that they saw no one inside the main living area of the house, a sprawling, high-ceilinged great room furnished with oriental rugs and ornate furniture. The scientist waved them on, jogging across the space with the three former SEALs and Fabi in tow. Except that, as they moved, it became apparent that Fabi wasn't really *in tow*, she easily kept pace with Maddock and the rest of them, running neck and neck with the scientist.

Bones caught up with her as they reached the opposite side of the room and turned into an arched hallway. "You feeling better, Fabi? Looks like you have more energy."

She eyed him with a smile and nodded. "I *do* feel better. Much better. Bones, what was that stuff you injected me with? Was it the experimental switch serum?" Her voice was edged with tension, with the unspoken fear that maybe Bones had managed to find some untested lab sample, and that it would wear off soon.

But he shook his head with an infectious smile. "Nope. Just good ol' sassafras."

"What?" They had to pause the conversation while they

ran down the hall and exited to an entrance room that led outside.

"You know, the plant sassafras. I noticed on the way through the lab, in the grow room part, that they had some, because my grandmother, a Cherokee Indian, used to use the stuff all the time for all kinds of ailments. She and her new age freaky friends still believe it can cleanse the blood and fight cancer. I've seen it work sometimes. So I ground it up with some saline solution and injected you with it. You know, figured there wasn't anything to lose."

He made eye contact with her as she drew him near. "And everything to gain." Their lips met until Willis yelled at them to get a room and the scientist shouted something unintelligible. Then Maddock fired a shot into the yard outside and Bones separated from Fabi, drawing his weapon.

"Don't let this go to your head, Bones but it's good to know you're good for something other than killing people. That being said, right now I need you to focus on killing people until we can clear a path down to the *Sea Foam*."

"Aye aye, Captain." Bones joined Maddock at the door leading out to the expansive backyard. The two of them crouched on either side of the doorway, reaching out to pepper the yard with rounds when they spotted muzzle flashes. Before long the opposition had been silenced, and Peter gripped Maddock by the shoulder.

"This is where we part ways." He pointed across the lawn to a rock-lined footpath leading through a landscaped area toward the ocean. "Take that path there until you get to a cliff viewing area, then take the stairs down to the dock."

Maddock extended a hand. "Thanks for your help, Peter. May your future employment decisions be made with more care."

The man nodded, pumped Maddock's hand and disappeared back into the house, where a cadre of *zombii* was involved in some kind of fracas with another one of Avila's men. Maddock led his friends through the yard, where they could hear vehicles arriving somewhere on the other side of the house. Maddock didn't know if they were Avila's reinforcements, local law enforcement or what, but he decided it was time for them to go, regardless.

The ragtag group made their way down the wooden stairway that zigzagged across the hillside until they came out on a rocky beach. A wooden walkway led to a pier, beyond which the *Sea Foam* still lay at anchor. They walked out onto the pier, and a short swim later, climbed aboard the boat.

Maddock started the engines and as they rumbled to life, Bones hauled in the anchor, a huge grin on his face as the sun began to set behind him. He paused in his anchor duties to look back toward the cockpit. "You know, Maddock, I have to admit. I think I may have found my true calling with this treasure hunting thing."

"I'm glad, Bones. But finish with the anchor so we can get out of here before someone decides they need us to answer a few questions."

Bones nodded and got back to his task while Willis took a seat in the cockpit. "So what happens now? Besides me patching up that shoulder, that is." He indicated the blood spot on Maddock's shoulder and opened a first aid kit.

Maddock took out a silver *real* he'd recovered from the fateful dive.

Willis eyed the coin with a sparkle in his eyes. "Hey, Maddock, you know what that coin's good for?"

He shot Willis a questioning look.

"A trip to Key West. Remember? You said if we found treasure, we'd stop in on the way back."

"That's right!" Bones backed Willis up from the bow.

"Seriously, though," Willis said, preparing to sew up Maddock's shoulder wound. "What's next, after that?"

Maddock smiled as he flipped the *real* over in his fingers, his eyes taking on a faraway look.

"Maybe we take another run at that treasure."

End

About the Author

David Wood is the author of the Dane Maddock Adventures and several other titles. Under his David Debord pen name he is the author of The Absent Gods fantasy series. When not writing, he co-hosts the Authorcast podcast. He and his family live in Santa Fe, New Mexico. Visit him online at www.davidwoodweb.com.